Contemporary Literatur

CW00401219

The Experience of the N
Primordial Soup – Christine de la Monica £8.99
Music, in a Foreign Language – Andrew Crumey £7.99
D'Alembert's Principle – Andrew Crumey £7.99
Pfitz – Andrew Crumey £7.99
The Acts of the Apostates – Geoffrey Farrington £6.99
The Revenants – Geoffrey Farrington £3.95
The Book of Nights – Sylvie Germain £8.99
The Man in Flames – Serge Filippini £10.99
Days of Anger – Sylvie Germain £8.99
Infinite Possibilities – Sylvie Germain £8.99
The Medusa Child – Sylvie Germain £8.99
Night of Amber – Sylvie Germain £8.99
The Weeping Woman – Sylvie Germain £6.99
The Cat – Pat Gray £6.99
The Black Cauldron – William Heinesen £8.99
The Arabian Nightmare – Robert Irwin £6.99
Exquisite Corpse – Robert Irwin £14.99
The Limits of Vision – Robert Irwin £5.99
The Mysteries of Algiers – Robert Irwin £6.99
Prayer-Cushions of the Flesh – Robert Irwin £6.99
Satan Wants Me – Robert Irwin £14.99
The Great Bagarozy – Helmut Krausser £7.99
Confessions of a Flesh-Eater – David Madsen £7.99
Memoirs of a Gnostic Dwarf – David Madsen £8.99
Portrait of an Englishman in his Chateau – Mandiargues £7.99
Enigma – Rezvani £8.99
The Architect of Ruins – Herbert Rosendorfer £8.99
Letters Back to Ancient China – Herbert Rosendorfer £9.99
Stefanie – Herbert Rosendorfer £7.99
Zaire – Harry Smart £8.99

Bad to the Bone – James Waddington £7.99
Eroticon – Yoryis Yatromanolakis £8.99
The History of a Vendetta – Yoryis Yatromanolakis £6.99
A Report of a Murder – Yoryis Yatromanolakis £8.99

The book entitled

: EROTICON :

Which
Contains most wondrous accounts
Concerning the nature of the erogenous parts and pudenda
Concerning erotic positions, discourses and reveries
And other such like:
And above all how each may endure
The sorrow of separation.
And moreover love potions and philtres
Yet also curses and spells of a most practical kind

From the hand of

YORYIS YATROMANOLAKIS
of Kreta

Dottore di Filosofia: Con licenza de'
Superiori, & Privilegio:

Done into plain English by
David Connolly

CANTABRIGIAE
MCMXCIX
PRINTED FOR THE PUBLISHING HOUSE OF *DEDALUS*

A HUMBLE THOUGH DELIGHTFUL WORK
DEDICATED
TO A MOST GENTLE AND ERUDITE
LADY
GRACIOUS IN EVERY WAY
WHO HAS OFT COMFORTED OUR PAST
AND SHALL RIGHTEOUSLY DECIDE THE FUTURE

Ἀφιερωθέν
εἰς τὴν Ελισάβετ
δέσποιναν πάνυ ἀμορόζαν
τὸ βιβλίον καλούμενον
ἐρωτικόν
(Translator's Respectful Dedication)

Table of Contents

On How This Book May Be Usefully Employed

Should you feel some urgency to digest this book, yet are beset by worldly concerns and cares, do not embark upon it in haste, since precipitance and impatience often lead to weariness and fatigue. Wherefore, select whichever chapters are most amenable to you (albeit that the substance of the book is singular throughout) and peruse these carefully, leaving the remainder for some other occasion. When again you find an opportunity, return to the matter in question, though be mindful that, just as leisure and idleness are most conducive to sexual intercourse and coition, thus also if your reading is to be productive, it requires tranquillity and concentration.

Should you be reading alone and suddenly your reading no longer affords you pleasure, abandon it forthwith and take up whatever else may be your heart's wish and desire. Should you be reading in the company of a lady (paramour or spouse) and you are suddenly overwhelmed by fantasy and desire, put the book down and set about the task that arouses and inflames you as you think fit. Upon finishing, assume again your composure and continue your perusal undistracted, even to a second and third respite.

When, God willing, you complete your reading of the book, do not place it indifferently and remissly on your shelves, as with your other books, but rather keep it beside your pillow, or in some other place to hand, and open it from time to time and peruse it at your will. And have with you a pencil to correct whatever errors you may encounter and to supplement whatever omissions or infelicities stemmed from the author's mind and hand. Yet sometime think of him too and grant indulgence for his toil and long and laborious nights.

To Intimates

Of all the wondrous things that nature has bestowed upon man (indeed on every living being), erotic love, viz. the desire for cohabitation and carnal union, is the most sublime by far and nothing more powerful exists or shall ever be found. Wherefore, even the Greeks of old (and Romans alike) did nought in their writings save sing praises to Eros and Aphrodite and eulogise love's joys and abundant delights. And if a man were to carefully peruse the sagacious texts of the ancients, he would compose numerous treatises pertaining to matters of love and great benefit would ensue to him in his life and common dealings. Yet not wishing to overly burden our present discourse and dull the treatise through an excess of erudition (not least vain sophistry), we shall (in support of our argument) humbly expound on but one or two of the many and exquisite things written by the Greeks on love. Thus, that most tender of elegists, Mimnermus of Colophon, in lamenting the irretrievable loss of love, declares that: Life is futile and devoid of all delight sans Aphrodite. Better then that I die the same hour that the secret liasons and clandestine embraces, love's couch and honeyed gifts cease to exist.

And Plato too, that amorous philosopher, much praises Eros and calls him a great and powerful god, declaring in his most enlightening Symposium *that of all the divine daemons, Eros is the most comely, most felicitous, yet also courageous and temperate. And he is comely for he pursues beauty, since like begets like, and he is gentle and his feet touch not upon the earth but alone step on mortal heads. He is, nonetheless, courageous since there is not one able to resist, no matter how he struggle and strive, wherefore he governs both gods and men. This and much besides is recounted in a panegyric of love by our philosopher and let no one neglect to carefully consider these things for he will reap great benefit thereby. And yet, let no one imagine that he will thus acquire the medicament for love through theory alone and the diligent study of these wondrous things. For though many are those who thus believed, the matter is yet not so, for the old and eternal adage holds true still, that Love has no medicament, nothing that can be imbibed, ingested or intoned, save only the bussing and claspings and the reclining of naked bodies.*

Yet, though many are the joys and pleasures of love, as many again, perhaps even more, are the pangs and torments it brings. And so great is the power that this daemon has over men and all things living, that very often strange and monstrous things are heard. Such as when, so it is said, certain animals of the Hyperboreans, known in their tongue as horsia and spotlessly white from the land's perpetual snows, are ready and ripe for mating, their sex so recedes that no one knows which are male and which female. They then begin to engage passionately in many long days of mating, whereupon after such prolonged union, they become one in flesh and never more separate, whether walking or grazing or sleeping. And if perchance someone imprudently sets out to harm them, these most sacred and lovelorn beasts take fright, becoming wild and frenzied, so that often, as has been witnessed, they fall furiously upon houses and farm buildings and entire towns have been destroyed on their account. And again, should someone chance upon them by misfortune, he will shed there and then his human form and be transformed into a wild horse. If, though, the horses are left in peace for the duration of their inordinate mating, little by little they become immaterial and ascend into the heavens and fly. And should their seed fall upon some spot, that place emits a fragrance and blossoms, and people recount certain inexplicable phenomena; to wit, that they see two or three suns thereabouts, though harsh winter and darkness prevail, and that they hear most melodious and amorous songs and much more besides.

And I presume that this is the meaning of the sacred words *Let them be one in flesh: that all creatures must join naked and consummate in their union so that they may conquer and surpass their divided state.* Yet reflect that the majority of us in our carnal cohabitation are sufficed by the superficial and by unions at once transient and fleeting. When, however, two bodies are destined for true cohabitation and encounter one another in full knowledge that they are the recipients of this gift, then the nature of things changes, becoming mysterious and awesome. And it is for reasons such as these that many young ladies feel suddenly lost and resign from their wedlock when, as in a dream, they encounter their true partner and surrender

14

to him. Others again grow wan and inexplicably fade and wilt like one demented as they ceaselessly cohabit with the unseen.

Such things as these and many more besides motivated me to compose the present work in which I have collected sundry matters gleaned from the writings of the ancients and of common benefit to intimates. This work I have entitled Eroticon, for I have set forth many and needful interpretations concerning love's sufferings and its sublime nature, concerning the sorrows to which it brings and obliges its victims, yet also concerning the affective benefits it affords to lovers both noble and bold. Certain writings I have transcribed in all fidelity from foreign scripts, others I have refashioned from older texts for our specific purposes, and others again I have conceived and elaborated upon out of my own needs and human constitution.

Be ever hale, Gentle readers

1.
Preface.
Concerning the Tripartite Composition of Bodies

In times long passed, when the nature of things was yet still gentle, supple and pliant, and all was fair, unsullied and rotund, humankind was but a single sex, monogenic and, in consequence, hermaphroditic. And this is attested not only by that most amorous of philosophers, Plato, but also by Holy Writ in the *Book of Genesis*, in which, as we are told, it is from the ribs of Adam that the first woman of the race is fashioned and thus called Eve, viz. she of the flesh. And that this gesture by the Supreme Being (to whom many attribute the illustrious nature of the divine) reveals mankind's original hermaphroditism, appears most plain if we but reflect on this one simple thing: how could the woman fashioned from Adam's ribs have acquired her natural sex if it were not that this same male flesh contains the female sex? When, however, time granted its consent and humankind became fixed as male and female, thereafter it was right that each should, as far as one is able, support and preserve one's own nature, unless it happens that some, as are indeed blessed, should possess the exceptional gift of embodied hermaphroditism, in which the holy angels alone rejoice and delight.

Meditating upon such things and more besides, and with the help of ancient and sacred works, I have resolved to set forth in this prefatory chapter the fundamental and eternal elements of the human body (of male and female alike), reflecting that many, who have not studied the matter as this humble writer has, may derive benefit from these writings, thereby attaining a deeper understanding of our true nature. For our natural disposition is not merely confined to what is plain to view, but extends to spheres both secret and concealed, and whosoever is knowledgeable of and enjoys familiarity with these shall reap joy and delight that is most erotic and aphrodisiacal, yet emotional and spiritual to boot.

The material elements composing every organism and living being are thus three in number: earth, or the cold element, the determining constituent of each one's body; water, which flows within us as a variety of fluids; and air, or the dry element, which infuses our limbs, animating and driving them. A fourth element common to all bodies, albeit immaterial and invisible, is fire, the same which kindles and warms the material elements, infusing them with life. And this life-giving fire has many aspects and is to be found in a variety of states as appears from its wondrous manifestations. For what else is man's spirit, the mind's spark and the soul's flame, if not one more aspect of the eternal fire of the universe entire? And again the passions that inflame and consume us, what do these reveal if not that we remain warm particles of the eternal world? And finally (not wishing to overly burden my discourse), what else is love and the desire for true and endless coition if not the living flame of our lives and our unquenchable thirst to cohabit with the other half? To one end: to consume and enkindle ourselves that our material elements may be freed from their shackles and that we may be fashioned anew as beings in utmost harmony and proportion. Since love, most gentle reader, is but our innate desire to refashion and rearrange our bodily parts anew through blissful and incessant coition (whether this be of a kind akin to earth, water or air) that our governing elements may be transformed and ring in accord with the heavenly and unsullied bodily parts of the angels.

The body thus having three natural elements, the main currents of love which govern these are also three. And at any one time, a body (be it male or female) is governed by the carnal element, at another by the fluidal, and at yet another by the aerial, or else spirited. Wherefore, analogous are also the places where love is born and flourishes, yet also the paths (manifest or clandestine) which it follows and where it disappears. Thus fervent lovers and those amorously disposed, prior to coition one with the other, are well-advised to study their own governing element and that of their cohabitator. For if in her ignorance an overly carnal woman cohabit and copulate with an overly liquid man and they give themselves imprudently to copulation *sine mente*, the man may well disintegrate due to the fleshliness of her vulva and suffer irreparable harm. The same may again happen should an overly fluidal man copulate, in his ignorance, and engage excessively in amorous struggle with a woman by her nature aerial. That is to say, from such a coupling, a tempest may arise that will assail and sink them both. If, however, before two bodies cohabit, they are at least aware of their governing element, this more than suffices in itself, and the cohabitation will prove not only greatly pleasurable but also most assuredly safe.

Notwithstanding, it is adjudged prudent for aerial to avoid cohabitation with aerial, carnal with carnal and fluidal with fluidal, and for them to interchange as oft as they are able, for similarity of elements and overly much in common soon creates satiety and the divine aspect and glow of the pudenda is slow to be achieved. Thus, in the case of two who are enamoured (or espoused) and who both possess aerial bodies, it is advantageous, yet also most agreeable, for one of them to turn to the sources of their fluids and to apply a modicum of such to the other. And in the instance where two unalloyed carnal or fluidal bodies unite, they should manage their bodies such that one of them libidinously discharges the missing element till they arrive by virtue of fire at the musical harmony of one flesh and substance.

2.
Concerning Pudenda and Erogenous Organs

Human pudenda are from the point of view of gender or sex three in kind: male, female and such as are in common, viz. the eyes, the mouth, the nose, the twenty-four extremities (being the total sum of legs, arms, fingers and toes) and others that each possesses by virtue of his nature or that he progressively acquires in his life. As regards conformation and aspect, the pudenda are of two kinds, that is the manifest and visible, and the undisclosed and unseen. It may well be, for example, that a fine man and bodily well-endowed numbers the sexual organs he possesses in accord with his knowledge and conjecture and therewith savours the delicacies of love. Yet he knows not that nature may have endowed him with other organs beyond those plain to view. Wherefore, it may come about that in some moment of ecstatic stoking or heavenly cohabitation, he encounters some newly-manifested pudenda and erogenous part of his body and is left in wonder.

As to their nature, pudenda are divided into two categories, viz. bodily and material or spiritual and immaterial, the first of which are referred by most writers of old as earthly and fleshly, the second as heavenly and notional. Yet, regardless of their nature, the essence remains the same and the nature of the erogenous organs is veritably material and immaterial. And however many material pudenda each man possesses, of equal number are his spiritual ones, so that the one corresponds to the other and is put to use depending on the moment and the need. Should it not be possible, for example, for one to physically touch his beloved (given that the lady happens to be far removed), well then, let him extend his heavenly and immaterial arm and fondle and burnish the desired body though it be at a distance of miles. And this is why love-stricken ladies at times feel an inexplicable thrill throughout their bodies and unconsciously assume a position *ala gato* (or even *ala cane*), ready to cohabit and to copulate till the roots of their hair turn red. And this comes about because they are roused and excited by the fingers of their lovers faraway.

And availing ourselves of the occasion, we shall refer briefly to what numerous older and also younger savants have observed concerning erotic matters: to wit, that every erogenous organ and human pudendum possesses all the senses, perhaps even more, that are normally to be found in every complete and integral body. That the hidden phallus and secret vulva feel and perceive by touch (even when garbed in their linen coverings) is well known to all. Yet, that the phallus hears or that the vulva sees afar, that it smells and savours the distant breeze, is comprehended by very few. And the more the venereal animation proceeds and intensifies, the keener the pudenda's senses grow and there are times that, though one has adjourned bodily, the eyes of the phallus remain wide open, or the hearing of the slumbering woman's crotch becomes so acute that she hearkens exceptionally well to things she is unable to apprehend in wakefulness. Know then these aspects of nature and pray be mindful of them, for if we have blind phalli and deaf vulvae, the pleasures that remain to us are but few indeed.

Finally, as to their sound and naming, pudenda may be called in numerous ways since each one refers to them differently and each land and region has its own names whereby one may delight in addressing and greeting them. For one venerates and greets his lady's vulva differently during the first hour of intercourse, differently again during the act of coition and yet again differently during frenzied copulation. And it is most wholly unbecoming (indeed impolite and uncouth) for one to address an inactive and impassive pudendum as O my gentle Vulva or O my sweet Cunnus, without this having been previously rendered consummate in its aphrodisiacal nature. Similarly, phallus is no aphrodisiacal word (for which reason physicians employ it) – yet the names verge or member are of a different nature. And if, finally, one wishes to copulate and close with his lady *de typo greco* (or contra natura), then he must first work thoroughly at her body's far orifice till it becomes ample and pliable. Whereupon let him call out to it,

O my Spiky Urchin, duct of my dreams, or O fount of unspeakable and vain, fruitless love. Yet if any incognizant fellow burns to enter into an unworked and unripe duct, knowing not how to call it and address it, well then, it were better that he abandon his endeavour at the portal, and climb into a cold and unworthy bath wherein he may abuse himself, alone and shivering, till he grunt and squirm as befits and merits him.

3.
Concerning the Gender of Angels

In a treatise from the land of Arabia, fashioned by the mystical brotherhood of the Rifa' i yi' Allaï, viz. the Guardians and Angel-struck, we have read most wondrous things such as these that follow:

Once the world, in both its visible and invisible aspects, had become fixed and ordered that it might receive the entire and irreducible number of living and lifeless bodies, it was filled at the same time by an equal number of heavenly and angelic essences, which total thousands upon thousands and myriad upon myriad, and still more again. Wherefore, every living body has its own angelic essence, which envelops and prudently guards it. And though each earthly body is identical with the essence of its angel, yet it differs in this one thing alone: that whereas the human pudenda are determined and distinctive, the sex of the angelic guardian is indistinct and undetermined. Thus every angelic form is able on the instant to become either male or female, or neuter or hermaphrodite. The task and duty of every living being, therefore, is to become like to its angel in sex, in accord with the example of the blessed brethren of the Rafa' i. The same who, having once reached the age for coition, exercise night and day that they might forget themselves amid the ecstasy of their interminable intercourse and the sundry couplings and postures whereby they progressively discard their singular sex and alternate from male to female unconcernedly. This said task is, however, greatly fatiguing and demands years of practice and study together with a religiously dedicated life.

Yet when one is rendered capable of this wondrous feat and, in life as in amorous discourse, becomes worthy of his cherubical hypostasis, he then acquires the mystical body of the angelic hosts, ascends into the heavenly vault and is able in this way more perfectly with fingers joined to stoke himself and others and shine radiant in a sacred, godly and supernal light. Should it happen, however, that this angel-struck fellow is

ever tempted and longs within his heart for his couch where-
on he was wont to cohabit as an earthly and mono-sexed
body, then (so it is reported) he is cast out from the order of
the dyadic and multi-sexed and, like to a fallen angel, must
commence the uphill path afresh.

ALL the aforementioned is, in our judgement, intensely
wondrous and astounding, yet unfamiliar and foreign to
our Christian nature, which, in concordance with our holy
doctrine, is, so it would appear, singular and unique. Moreover,
an awesome and indisputable proof is that at time of holy
christening when we are lain entirely open before men, we
assume one single name corresponding to our visible sex.

4.
Concerning Venereal Union and Matters Appertaining thereto

If in truth you would become and be reckoned as an able lover and amorist and most seasoned in love, then accustom yourself each day to observing the many and varied erotic practices to be found in the world of nature (among all living creatures, no matter whether of earth, water or air) and strive to imprint them well and deeply within you and to oft repeat them in practice and in reverie. For then love's abundant gifts will be revealed to you and you shall have much gain and benefit for your needs. Only such as are ignoble in erotic matters and uncouth believe they possess full knowledge and are unable to learn. Yet the matter is of vital concern, as is known to the most noble and impassioned of lovers, and for this very reason they daily strive for libidinous enlightenment and engage in unceasing practice. This, as is said, is what the renowned Paris did all day, the same who through his erotic arts destroyed two kingdoms and countless legions. And the Hellene, Alcibiades, so we are told, had practical knowledge of three score ways and positions *di amore*. And lest anyone think that the noble art of loving was known only to the ancients, mention must be made of our own Yoryis Karaiskakis, who could at one time serve five persons (women and men alike) without in any way tiring his verge or losing his stride. Whence did this uncultivated, albeit most noble, fellow obtain such knowledge and dexterity unless from nature, our one true master and counsellor?

Thus, of the many and varied venereal unions, we shall refer to but three examples and let the prudent man dwell on these. How many, then, are aware that nature has provided its creatures with the gift of being able to cohabit (should they so wish) not only through contact between their multifarious pudenda, but also through other parts of their bodies which ostensibly are devoid of erogenous matter. Hence, it has been observed that a certain genus of parakeet with wondrous plumage and most human in voice, known as *sittaca somniala* and from the reaches of Brazil, employs its back to effect sexual contact. Indeed, during the mating season (with the start of the New Year or Primavera), their genitals begin to acquire a lustre and to glow enticingly even at a great distance. Whereupon, all these lovelorn and wind-borne creatures congregate and once they have arrived at sexual passion by displaying their lustre, they most diligently fuse their backs and quite slowly proceed to merge the one with the other till their bodies are absorbed and glow with fire. And when, anon, one begins to emerge from the other side and they are rendered separate, they once again face each other in accord with nature, join their pudenda and the union is concluded.

A similar occurrence can be noted in the spotted eels of the South Seas which are lacking in visible pudenda. Thus, during the time of mating, though they ever journey in pairs and swim in parallel, they suddenly halt in most marvellous fashion and turn to face each other. And after admiring and amorously gazing at each other for a sufficient length of time, the female opens her mouth and allows the male to slowly enter until he is completely ingested. And when the male reaches the female's fragrant ovary, he spits out his sperm as saliva over the eggs that they may be fertilised and then continues his course till he emerges through the female's rear. And once he has emerged, he barely manages to turn and lie with his mate, exhausted from the profound pleasure, since he has given birth and been given birth to at one and the same time.

A third most bizarre erotic phenomenon (yet most instructive for the amorous) can be observed in our own lands, and particularly in the southerly isle of Kreta. There is in that place a genus of most wondrously-breeding weasel (*nymphe cretensis*) which, at a certain time and when in heat (aided by the isle's fair winds) unites in earth and in flesh with the male not by means of the visible pudenda, but heel to heel and sole to sole. The two creatures, so it is said, lie down and bring the soles of their feet together, rubbing them so softly and persistently that before too long they are most desirously aroused and behave as if in frenzy. And should someone chance to pass by at that moment, he will perceive a greatly intoxicating fragrance and himself will acquire sexual abilities beyond the natural bounds. It would seem that from this kind of union are derived the Kretan forms *to soleate* or *to besole*, which denote coupling till the blood runs dry. Others again call this practice *heeling* or *heelation*, though it is uncertain whether this does indeed refer to the coupling of weasels as previously expounded, or quite simply means to vigorously mount a lady and spur her flanks with the heels till she emits abundant froth and a mighty groan.

5.

Concerning Erotic Positions and Couplings

As is remarked by those well-versed in such matters, the positions for love-making available to the human species are unlimited and each one is able to discover and savour as many as his heart desires. The most common and pleasurable, nonetheless, are three score and twelve in number according to some and four score according to some others. Yet this sum refers but to one pair of bodies, for if more than two persons practise intercourse together, it is plain that the number of positions is thereby multiplied. This humble writer is unable to testify to more than forty positions and conjoinings. Notwithstanding, these are not few in number and are more than is necessary, so that a detailed explanation of each may cause some to grow impatient on account of verbosity and overly much description. Wherefore, we shall content ourselves with mentioning but a few forms of erotic conjoinings from the so-called alphabets of old, which are at once the most facile and most easily remembered for the diligent and studious. Whosoever would learn more, let him do so of his own accord and sample others.

Many are those who know certain innocent love verses, which, commencing as they do alphabetically and proceeding in the order of the letters, have thus been called Alphabets of Love. Yet few are aware that the true Alphabet of Love relates first and foremost to erotic couplings and carnal conjoinings and not to innocent love games. Consider but the shape of the capital letters in Greek (no less in other tongues), and you shall straightway grasp the meaning.

The letter A (Alpha), first as it is in the order of the alphabet, also denotes the first position of practical and intelligible coition, though it requires great dexterity and patience. Take hold, then, of your lady (paramour or spouse), the two of you freshly bathed and clean, and lay her stark naked on the couch of your coition. Having well lubricated her that she may be flexible and moist, have her bend into two parts (equal or unequal as you wish) and hold her arms outstretched as in prayer and her legs likewise. Yet take care that her upper mouth and lips correspond to her lower lips and well-springs. Then come upon her laterally between her outstretched arms and legs, inscribing thus the letter A. If you delight in concealed fluids, from fount and fundament, affix yourself in this position and imbibe thereof, having your verge directly turned upon her head and tongue. If you long for the founts of her saliva, turn about and set to your nuzzling, yet ram your rod where it most inflames you that the letter may be thus approximately joined. In this way, the A of love is formed, either through contact between the upper and lower pudenda, or by means of the mouth, or by the nape and the heels, yet also by the eyes and remaining senses, providing that a little order and calligraphy are employed. Also possible is the alteration and recomposition of the letter in which it is the male who bends as the base and the female who entwines herself and joins with him in the way aforementioned.

The Greek letter B (Beta) also denotes an erotic position, one most profound yet most virile. Should you prefer to inscribe the B horizontally whereby you constitute the spine and your lady the outward side, then lie down straight, being naked and clean, and taking up your lady's body, place it upon you snake-like so that it rests upon the head, verge and heel. Should you wish to move now in snake-like fashion, then set to and straighten your lady, either with lips and pudenda corresponding or conversely. Inscribed upright, the letter B is most erotic, albeit difficult and even impossible for the unversed. Yet whosoever enjoys learning assimilates it easily and those versed in the same enjoy great pleasure since (as is said) they are suspended in ecstasy and in their mind's void and think their veins to be transparent, as now their fluids flow down in torrents from their head and now ascend wondrously and preternaturally from their legs to their crown.

The Greek (Gamma), hence gamahuche, denotes a most difficult position and requires considerable practice and an innate flame, for otherwise the shape soon dissolves and loses its relish. Thus, prior to attempting the Gamma, take care to proceed as follows: take up your lady and bare her to her innermost parts and lubricate and warm her well till she becomes smooth and soft to your satisfaction. Thence (following four hours of spittling and tongue-play), set her on the floor either straight and lengthwise, or doubled and well-bent. If she is straight, then double yourself with precision and proceed to bind yourself to her head, either that she may suckle you as in the style of Madonna and Infant, or that you may sprinkle her with hyssop and secret myrrh. If again she is set doubled and bent, then assume your full length and finely attune yourself, either attaching yourself to the one side and drawing from her burning well-spring, or climbing to the place of her crown, and insinuate your tool into her mouth. Yet ever maintain the letter's shape for the sake of good order. The upright Gamma is achieved in like manner, though this same requires great diligence in body and mind and whoever succeeds at this is thereafter known as Gamesome and Gamic.

The easiest and at once most gratifying is the Greek letter O (Omicron) whereby the amorous couple curl gladly and idly the one around the other and copulate ceaselessly and pleasurably. As for the remaining capital letters, betake yourself in like fashion and inscribe them well and prudently.

6.
Concerning Womanly Types and How to Avoid Harm During Coition with the Same

As has been remarked by the ancients, the types of women in relation to the conformation and aspect of their pudenda are five, whereas the male gender was fashioned uniformly and ingenuously. Wherefore, it is wise to study the female types for you shall procure great benefit therefrom.

The ancients thus determined the five female types as follows: those like to mammals, viz. the cat-like, the hare-like and the horse-like, and a further two like to the species of insects and of birds, viz. the spider-like and the dove-like. And this is apparent from the pudenda: the cat-like woman has comely, foliaceous pudenda, ample in size and most gratifying and delectable in smell and taste, moist and like in nature to the whole body. And their charm is that prior to becoming aroused and resplendent, they appear quite demure and reserved, yet once given the opportunity, they fully reveal themselves and gleam like a cat's claws. And herein lies the danger. For when you come to this spring, o weary traveller, take care in no way to spoil or stir the water, but on the contrary, allow it to come out and flow plentifully and gladly that you may be quenched. Prostrate yourself then as does the pilgrim, bow low, reverently kiss and embrace the genitals, yet neither ram nor rummage. Wait till her genitals move in and out at will and take account of when they do so truly and not deceptively, then clutch at them most tightly. And if they remain thus, it is a clear sign that your lady has passed from a sham to a sure position and that you shall have carnal union and not merely a sense of coition. Thereupon, and after not a little time has elapsed, stoke her in staccato fashion and work things thus and manipulate the situation to your greater benefit that you may avail yourself of at least seven positions and couplings. For such is required of this vulva's foliage if it is to be sucked dry.

The hare-like woman recalls the hare, which has yet hides and which exists yet secretly and surreptitiously emerges. And the pudenda of such like are foliaceous and most fragrant, yet the inner labia are eggshell fine and fragile, therefore take care when in contact and when rummaging. And since her charm is that she straightway openly discloses her pudenda yet conceals and covers them *in progresso* (an instinctive precaution), you risk being thwarted and cut off in full flow. Wherefore, first lavish her with blandishments for six hours and ply her with words (falsehoods for truths and truths for falsehoods) and first extract from her the Good Water that, without fear, she may regain her clarity and thence take hold of her key and move it slowly, up and down, till it unlocks of its own accord (and not through compulsion). Assume then the position of the humble supplicant and repeat these words: "come, come my comely" and cradle her as her mother might, below the arms, *destro e sinistro*, and grasp her well and boldly, till she finally tires and her foliage opens wide. Required positions at least eleven.

The horse-like type reveals the pudendum's ardour, yet also the size and state. And since the horse-like type possesses moist, shifting and transient pudenda, it is proper that her paramour (yet also her spouse) should ever assume the position of an inverted and balancing rider. For their charm is that they induce fantasy and reverie, yet also despondency and grief. Thus, it would seem prudent prior to your contact with such women to learn the so-called Mongolian riding whereby, at time of orgasm, these lovelorn cavaliers mount an unbroken and untamed mare, keep their balance with one foot on the mare's croup and, while holding their genitals in the conjugal position, cry out melodiously yet most plaintively "Allah-i, Allah-i!".

The spider-like type denotes the pudendum's odium and corruptibility, for such a woman has double genitals and while you are working the one, the other comes and catches you off-guard. It also denotes the polyandry of her nature, for she has many scaffolds set up around her like a spidery warp which hangs on the air to trick and deceive. And since her gift is seduction and the musical allure of her bosom, seal the redundant ears of your phallus that you may not be caught feckless. And once you have animated her with utmost reverence and *molto determinato* and ritually crossed her pudendum, commence ramming her from her outer parts and thresh liberally all about her. Next, assume the position of the cock when it writhes under the knife and drive your peg in direct and deep. Thereupon discharge your seed in reams and withdraw with care and caution. Yet if you find yourself faint from so much discharge, then sit and patiently await judgement and the gnashing of teeth.

The dove-like type is clear so as to require no interpretation. It denotes that though this type flies and hovers just as the other female types, it behaves like to the doves which feed from you yet defecate upon and soil you. Notwithstanding, this type is most fair and greatly erotic and takes pleasure in the main coition *ala verso*, and in the second crouching one, *ala traversa*. Yet be not deceived by appearances and affability, for many have been thus deluded and came to harm. Wherefore, before coming upon these same, draw out your fingers to the point of pain and render them longer and dexterous in grappling at far remove. Next, place your beloved in the position of a seated sphinx and, should she cast a sharp glance, appease her appropriately. Rummage her only when she indicates to you that she is truly inflamed and acts like a dove in heat. Thereupon, assume a cautionary position and press her flanks using your thighs and work her soundly. Discharge then prematurely, thereby to ascertain whether she is content, and thence begin in the way of domestic cats that pluck birds clean and finish airily though prudently. And ever feed her with your one hand and offer her enticing seeds, that she may sit meekly and willingly, for otherwise you set yourself at risk. This being the case, rather than suffer harm, abandon your efforts and ply yourself without pity.

These, then, in summary, are the womanly types, such that each man may commit them to memory and avail himself of them. Yet bear in mind, gentle reader, that the majority of women (if not all), regardless of their dominant type, possess all the other types in embryo and correspondingly reveal and employ them. Wherefore, take extra care in the satisfaction of your needs and be not deceived, but train yourself and study the matter in practice and in reverie, that you may be gratified and gratify, harmlessly and happily.

7.
On How to Make the Acquaintance of Comely Women and Charm Them to Your Advantage

Comely and most delectable women are everywhere discernible and plentiful. Yet eyes and hearts to recognise and enslave them are but few. Therefore, should you indeed wish to discover and acquire for your own account these shapely creatures that all year long hover around streets and squares in happy song, then follow diligently all such as is set out below, which has been tried and tested by generation upon generation of amorous men, all of whom found consummate satisfaction.

Choose whatever time of year you wish, whether night-time or daytime is of no consequence. Enter your bathroom and first wash meticulously and diligently all parts of your body, manifest and unmanifest, inside and out. Carefully bathe and clean the eyes of your body yet also of all your pudenda (in no way neglecting the eyes of your fingers, nose, tongue or heart) and, to the best of your ability, illumine all the secret centres of your mind. Emerge thus in your doorway, bathed, spruced and perfumed, yet also with a heart that is clean and unsullied. Then take out your kerchief of desire (the same that every man keeps carefully concealed within him) and tie it either around your neck or pin it firmly upon your breast. If you are fond of a cigarette or plain tobacco, light one and inhale it as you please. If again you prefer simply an inner song, do not voice it lest it lose its charm in the breeze: allow it to float over your inner lips and it shall be heard, whether you sing out or not.

When, anon, six hours of the clock have passed and you have the taste of poppy (*cioé opio tebaico*), whether standing in your own doorway or in some corner of the square, or before the church steps, or wherever else your fancy may take you, turn your cleansed eyes swiftly in all directions and survey the view. Should you see passing by a woman plain to most (perhaps even to her own self), regard her in full light and admire her as if she were most comely and deeply desirable to you (for in truth she is) and call to her from within you, humming either the song of the scorned or the hymn to the unjustly slain. Thereupon she will turn all her radiance upon you and all the disconsolateness surrounding her (she being supposedly plain) will dissolve and disappear. It is then that in similar fashion you must reveal to her all your graces and virtues, affective and physical, and recite for her delight the song of those beloved and forlorn. And if anon you say to her "Come, follow me my most precious," she will come in haste, and if you say to her "bare yourself, my fair young lady, and reveal all to me," she will bare herself without more ado, revealing to you her most hidden parts albeit in the midst of the square or street. And if you say to her, "Prostrate yourself, my dearest, that I might enter you and ride and rummage you till the roots of your hair turn red," she will prostrate herself at your desire and your joy will be consummate.

If again you should find yourself idle and languorous for six hours of the clock, do not yet despair. For, most suddenly, while you are repeating the song of the scorned rider and are thick with smoke and sullen, the atmosphere will clear, as in a flash of joy, and passing before your eyes you will espy a fair woman, gliding and resplendent, such an one as you sought in the years of your youth yet never chanced upon, or one you secretly admired for no less than seven years, without ever becoming deserving of her. Wherefore, cast aside your melancholy and reveal to her most clearly all the parts of your body, all your inner and outer fingers, even your rings, the same which you wore for her in your heart of hearts and on your limbs on account of your subservience and devotion to her, and softly say to her (that you may be deeply heard) "O, you, my Reverie, incarnate and unfashioned by hand, behold how for seven years I cleansed and purified myself on your account. No longer hold yourself so high and haughty, but fly closer to the ground. For now the time has come for me." And forthwith she will cast her radiance upon you and will cease her flight. And she will assume a lascivious pose and will succumb to you *molto volontieri* and with relish and she will prostrate herself for you *allegra con foco* and unlaced. And you will mount her as you are (clean and unsullied) and ride her and ram her thoroughly and spiritedly, no less than seven hours of the clock, genuinely and deeply till the final stentorian groan.

8.
On How to Copulate on Water without at all Sinking

Fashion a sheet from fibres of sea lilies (*giglia di mare*), six feet in length and five in breadth, and on it embroider a calm and tranquil sea of blue. Next, take numerous stopples, or small corks, round and smooth ones, and sew them into the borders of the cloth. Thereafter find a stretch of sea, secret and hidden from view, facing south, and proceed until standing firmly and safely on the sand. Spread the sheet on the water and allow it to unfold with the ripples until it opens out and floats. This done, endeavour to climb upon it and squat alike to a musing fellow who, sitting cross-legged, is smoking a narghile, and take care that the sheet in no way wrinkles or creases. If you find this unimaginable and beyond your powers, do not lose heart; for reflect that here you will lie with your lady in elemental copulation, wherefore attempt it again and yet again, till you become accustomed and achieve your goal.

Thus, when well-rehearsed and confident of success, take your lady and make for the shore, saying to her "Come, dearest, and assist me in spreading my sheet on the sea". And when she accompanies you, mount the sheet in the way you have learned and let the corks hold you secure and afloat. Then draw up your lady and place her crouching in the very centre of the cloth and have her bare herself completely till her seven fluids appear and spill into the brine and turn white. And once you see white sea foam appearing all around, fragrant from the liquids of her springs, make her kneel in the midst of the sea and ride with her in the way of reptiles, that coil and stretch, and again coil and stretch. While doing this, sing to your own rhythm the shanties of the old seafarers, such an one as, "Yo-heave-ho, yo-heave-ho . . .". Whereupon, having rowed well and the ripples on the water having grown larger, come and ram your lady deeply, two and three times, or as your capabilities allow. Yet take care, as you ram and make like a pirate for the inner bays and coves, lest she become sea-sick and dizzy from the sea and grow tired and weary on you. Then (when the wind and turbulence abate) take up the sheet and wrap her in it well for the sake of propriety and the damp and make speed and head for the deserted shore. There set down your lady and take her in your embrace and give her the folded sheet to keep, until your next voyage.

In a most enlightening treatise from India, we have read that this wondrous thing can also take place on lakes and rivers. And, as in that blessed country there is in nature infinite lengths and breadths of navigable waters, so it happens that lovers cover many miles travelling upon their tiny sheets and render a spectacle both pleasing and instructive to a plethora of people.

YET, if one should marvel and wonder at this, what will he say on hearing this other? For it is reported that certain nomads, most amorous ones, from beyond the North, are able to copulate on a suspended sheet at an elevation of seventy feet or more, and on which the well-practised can rise to a height of one thousand feet, mating in a most frenzied manner. How this happens, I do not know, but I do not deny the truth of it, given love's power and its indomitable force. Rather, I liken the whole matter to what certain birds called windmaters do in the lands of the Greeks. These exquisite birds can be seen hovering motionless for hours in the air in a passionate frenzy and mating with the wind. And from their great shaking and their ecstatic flapping, they shed a huge number of feathers and in no way cease till they are completely exhausted and plummet lifeless to the ground. I am at a loss to understand what these demented birds sow and reap in the heavens. Yet for them to behave thus, as decreed by nature and the Almighty, there must be some true purpose, albeit incomprehensible to man.

9.
On How to Copulate with a Lady Before Her Husband Without His Being Aware of You

Should you be for a length of days unsaddled with your seed untapped and unable to obtain a woman both willing and amenable to your needs, yet you are tormented by your spermal fluid, betake yourself as follows and you shall find relief albeit temporary. Rise up at an early hour and, after performing your ablutions inside and out, go over to your window facing South and give praise to your Lord that you have once more seen the light of day today. Thereafter, take two pinches of dried lily dew (*acqua di giglio*), four ounces of bitter almond oil and seven ounces of prime essence of royal mint and apply them well to the genitals for fragrance and for fervour. Afterwards, dress fittingly in your best and festive apparel and enter into an erotic fantasy, as a hermit might enter the Almira desert. Yet neither boast of your passion nor proclaim it, but prudently conceal it. At some bright midday hour, take yourself out for a stroll and sit alone and treat yourself to whatever be your wont. If what you desire is a strong cigarette or fine tobacco cigar, indulge yourself in moderation. If you desire a beverage of strong liquor, partake cautiously thereof. Then, before being burned by the sun and roasted in the desert, rest your eyes and dwell on the idea that a vehicle is supposedly transporting you on a journey far from your land, along a vast and blazing road. This same denotes wandering love.

Then two persons will appear before you, supposedly fellow travellers, a charming and well-matched couple, lately wed with religious rites. Let him be approximately thirty three years of age and she have at least twenty four years behind her, for it is then that the woman's fluids and juices are released in their full fragrance. If your preference is for dark shades of hair, though a lily skin, unadorned and resplendent, then paint her thus. If your delight is in white and russet, then let this be how you fashion her. Give no concern to the colour of her garments, whether pure white or mauve or crimson is of no consequence. Yet give care to the quality. Without ado, let her outer garment be of linen, of cotton or Cathay silk, this being most agreeable to the touch and worn close to the body for ease of access.

Thereupon, and while the vehicle is shaking you *andante*, once more pray reverently to your God and take out from your innermost parts either an eye's hand, or a finger's nose or a tongue's ear, cleansed as ever and sensitive. Then recline on your seat in the position of a man seated *ala libido con fellatio* and fix your gaze on the lady facing you, inconspicuously yet most carnally, reflecting on which of her parts might most easily open to view. If you discover that it is her arm's niche, arm yourself, if her knee, kneel before her, if her neck, become her necklace and, with feigned innocence yet speedily and adroitly, cover her with all your limbs so that wherever she perspires, there will you insert your fingers and refresh them, wherever she quivers, quiver with her in unison. Whereupon, having pressed yourself close to her and made her your possession, insinuate your notional hand still further betwixt her thighs and breasts and wander ever inwards, reclining and in all humility, as though you were taken up with the journey and fatigued. Let them engage each other in talk and ignore you.

When the afternoon has run its course and the sun is right for setting, moisten the finest of your fingers either in your spittle or in the fluid of your member and lubricate it till it is fully come loose and, thus freed of flesh, insert it into the gaping crevice between her thighs. Yet take care not to come face to face with her pudendum lest you be perceived. First come upon her laterally and from the right beneath the selvage of her linen and wait. For if one finger stealthily enters, then a second and third will follow. Come upon her in similar fashion from the left and enter from there too, thence lightly grasp her linen wherever it most becomes you and pull it gently though adroitly *e molto determinato*, leaving her wholly naked though seated.

Should you then wish to smell her linen, do so; if taste is your preference, so avail yourself, yet do not imprudently grow faint, but put the linen to your breast that it may beset you. Then gather all your smell and smell her throughout, bring your entire hearing close and listen to her and release all your suckers upon her and drain her to the last drop of blood and milk.

Anon (when, weary from the journey, the one reclines upon the other), come up beside her *con salto d'amore* and thus eagerly arrange her legs and thighs, and equally intently squeeze her breasts and nipples that her two upper lips may open and, as though a breeze of nostalgia or drops of imagined milk and honey were pouring out, she may rain her breath upon you.

And when, finally (night having fallen), you see her closing her heavy eyes and becoming distant, then stoke her from below, thereby opening and plundering her underground caverns till she grows disconcerted, shaking throughout her body, and turns to her sire in bewilderment and fear. Do not then be sparing with the scents, nor work your member frugally and intermittently, but discharge yourself fully and completely and proffer her your mystical and haloed glans, for another's beloved, indeed one present, gladdened you and attended to you in your desolation. And when you finish your task, give her once again into the arms of her spouse, naked and quivering as one unshackled, remove her linen from your breast and place it afresh around her inner recesses. Then collect yourself decorously and be on your way.

10.
On How to Copulate with a Lady on Horseback or on an Ass' Foal

If you are equestrian by nature and betaken with the ethos of cavaliers and horsemanship, yet also in erotic matters you reckon yourself capable and erudite, then do as set out here and you shall rejoice doubly and trebly. Yet, take great care during the undertaking for the same is most dangerous and, for the unversed and untrained, may prove at once risible and profane.

Take the finest of your horses, whether white or black is of no consequence, and train it to canter finely and gracefully, with head erect. Yet also to keep its back most steady and unshaking as it goes, be the terrain gentle or steep. Then take up your lady (paramour or spouse) and set out with her on riding trips of as many as a dozen in number. Commence with the horse well-saddled and sit with her in a single saddle, astride or sidesaddle as you wish, but make sure your genitals are aglow and swing innocently while cantering. Once you have grown accustomed to these jaunts, unsaddle the horse and, with boldness and liberty, set your lady upon it entirely naked underneath (though outwardly in fine and colourful attire) either against your flesh or that of the horse. Yet have no thought to ram her, even should you burn in front, nor to feverishly clasp her buttocks if these same shine from the rear. For do as the noble and amorous knights in the wilderness who extend their right hand and clutch their air's mane and show their left hand empty and plaintive, that supposedly they are holding tight their incorporeal and dreamlike damsel.

Await the bright and blazing afternoon and, taking your horse, curry and scrub it thoroughly that it may again more cleanly perspire. Next, wash your own self and likewise your lady and lubricate yourself from her and lubricate her in similar fashion, to and fro. Mount with her, all of you unharnessed, and make for the nearest bower where are to be found abundant trees, herbage and blossoms and violets and fragrant blossoms. And ask that streams of cool water may flow all around and fertile plots and orchards may shine forth before you. Then set her to ride either turned away from you (for stoking *ala recto*) or vice-versa (for stoking *ala verso*). If you feel yourself to be in fine fettle and clean, get her to sit behind you and press against you either with her nipples erect or with her wet croup. And when you are thus arranged, give whip and spur to the horse till it adopts a natural and airy elevation.

Once you have run around the area greatly inflamed and delight both in the breeze and the fragrance of the fruit, the moment will arrive when your beads of perspiration will appear and merge as one, yet too the roots of your pudenda will be loosened and will curl against the sheen of the horse's coat. Then assume a handstand on the horse, as the able and practised rider that you are, and adhere your lips either to your lady's vulva or to her darkest duct, which running wet, rubs and licks against the back bearing you both. Whereupon, endeavour to close your legs around the nape of her neck whether you be in front or behind. Do this moreover to protect and subjugate her body that where she has her head, there your end is turned.

When you have imbibed well of the water and of your perspiration and you see horse and lady rider quivering together with you, give the whistle for perpetual and harmonious movement and steer your horse that it may rise up and sail smoothly on the breeze. And when your steed's back is inundated by aromas and its genitals rattle in the air, place your lady wholly prostrate (though supine will do as well) with her head towards either the animal's mane or tail. There, set her in equilibrium and bestride the horsewoman horseman-like and stoke her while riding and windswept and ram her ceaselessly and tirelessly two and three and four times, if, languishing, she deems you worthy and offers herself. Thereupon, as you breezily discharge, you will feel the spray from the horse's noble seed engulfing and anointing you and likewise the spray of the woman.

Then give praise to your Lord that he granted you to copulate and discharge there where only the most pure and hawk-weaned copulate, and cross yourself in thanksgiving

70

and give voice to some old and suitable hymn. And when late in the evening you return anew to the bower from the heavens, you will see that where first there were leaves, now flowers bloom and what blossomed before now bears most delicious fruit. Take then your steed and woman and allow them to rest and feed them well and lavishly. Next place your lady against the horse's bosom and lull them both to sleep gently and most softly, and lay your own self beside them and keep watch in the wondrous garden till morn.

The same may also be undertaken on an ass' foal. Yet since this beast is not alone capable of elevated flights, curry the humble beast well that it may shine as much as possible, and strap to its sides seven holy date palms, viz. sacred palm branches, to serve as wings and hold it up. Then set your lady upon the ass thus prepared and carry out all the afore-mentioned, praying devoutly as you rise to the heavenly passion.

11.
Concerning Erotic
Scents and Odours

B e wary for erotic scents are of sundry kinds, so that one unversed may easily confuse and spoil them through want of experience. Wherefore, many older perfumers and apothecaries (from East and West) have striven to distinguish these in practical fashion for the benefit of diligent amorists. Thus, in a certain and most useful treatise from Greece, entitled Dioscurideion, we find that in fact all erotic aromas are of five types, divided according to the corresponding parts of the body, viz. 1. the ethereal scent of the breath; 2. the heady scent of saliva and perspiration; 3. the viscous scent of the sealed pudenda; 4. the effusive scent of the open pudenda; and 5. the notional scent of virginity. If, therefore, you desire to procure aromatic essence for your every need, yet are inexperienced and unversed, first commence with one source of erotic odour and once accustomed and adept, proceed then to obtain the rest. Bear in mind, however, that only very few are able to employ all the aromatic substances at once, on account of sensitivity of smell, yet also of the danger and drowsiness brought on by an overly large number of scents.

Since then love is by nature perfumed and guileless and is averse to all things sullied or tainted, before you attempt any erotic perfumery, thoroughly cleanse both body and soul. First enter your bathroom and meticulously wash all your bodily parts with pure and plentiful water, yet take care also to cleanse your heart and likewise your mind. Remain in your moisture without towelling till you are dry and thereupon take a branch of sea lily (Pancratium maritimum) and shake it crosswise throughout the air of your existence, to the fore, to the rear and at the sides, avoiding to let it touch your flesh for sake of the flower's pride. Upon completing your ablutions, call the lady of your reveries and dreams and bathe her similarly, washing her entirely, outwardly and inwardly, and blow the warmth of your breath over her body till she be dry. Thereupon, take her reverently and set her wholly naked on a couch draped in white and unblemished by the amorous ardour of others.

Smell her thus entirely and deeply for two or three hours of the clock and imbibe most thoroughly her body's three airs, the sanguineous, lacteal and fluidal, and intoxicate yourself thereby as one who is bemused or demented. Once you have smelled her thoroughly and lubricated her flesh with your saliva, select the scent that most becomes you and have with you a glass phial, of gentle colour, that you might place it in the corresponding flow, whether it be in the perfumed mouth or the angelic armpits, or the moist vulva, or wherever else it pleases you. Yet be sure, when tapping the scent from the source that attracts you, not to ignore the remaining parts, neither mentally nor physically, and either smell them as they exhale of their own accord, or move your fingers in the petals of their organs thereby animating them.

If, then, your penchant is for the mouth's breathings and sighs, let your lady lie entirely open and reverently insinuate your verge either to the deepest level of her duct or to the load line of her vulva and work it inside all her clefts and lips, that they may move harmoniously and yearn for you. Thus, as the lower lips open, so also, as has been observed, the upper ones open correspondingly, and as the lower tongue breathes and flutters and drips its fluids, so too the tongue in her mouth. Thereupon, plant your entire verge upright wherever you so please and drive it thus that the lower air may be sealed and begin to flow upwards and bead by bead begin to course through her body. Hold then the phial at the edge of her mouth and, as the exhalations issue from her depths, fill it with the ethereal scent of the upper breath.

Should you wish to collect the odour from her hermetically sealed pudenda (known also as Mary Magdalene's myrrh), first make a cross over the airs of your lady's flesh and thrice notionally inscribe the words *Kyrie Eleison* that the essence of the scent may not spoil and lose its savour. For just as the Lord is praised and worshipped with pure incense, this similarly befits the worship of love. Whereupon, take a white undergarment, linen and unworn, and wave it over the sealed pudenda softly chanting and spitting to drive away any impure air hovering and adulterating the smells. Thereupon, as you have your instrument well tuned, insert this same (after turning with all propriety) either between the lines of her teeth or into the folds of her palate and keep it there sealed and silent for a goodly length of time. As she drains and nuzzles you on high, for your part titillate her below (having her correspondingly reversed) till the lower pores warm and blaze like the earth's craters and you see, rising from the pudenda, a white air, sweet incense and sacrifice before you. Then fill the phial with the essence and pure scent and keep it for times that are cold and odourless.

Do this with the remaining scents in combinatory manner. And always have with you the replete phials of odours and, in your every need, open them, smell and give praise to their source. And if (ever) your perfumer denies you and betakes herself to other perfumeries and couches one fine day, and presents herself to you proud and aloof, the moment you espy her from afar, come up to her and fall to the ground and, taking the phial with her scents of old, shatter it at your lady's feet as a token of worship and subservience. And she will be assailed within by indescribable desire and either she will stoop to gather you up, languishing as you are in the dust and the dirt, or she will don the old scent you produced together and will dissolve with this into the air.

As for the notional scent of virginity, it is said that this is highly difficult to collect, for, though every single body possesses a source of virginal perfume, very few are aware of this and make provision for it. Wherefore, should you ever find yourself in a virginal aperture, be mindful of the difficulty of the task and have with you many phials and fill them. Then avail yourself of the perfume either alone or in company.

12.
Concerning Aphrodisiacal Dishes

Many believe that in order to acquire a most virile and able appetite *calor naturale*, viz. an inner ardour for matters aphrodisiacal, it is necessary to partake of the appropriate foodstuffs, which they seek to no avail. And notwithstanding that the ancients have recorded certain edibles and beverages facilitating the flow of sperm and fluids, the matter is somewhat different. How else may one interpret the lack of aphrodisiacal urges in healers and physics who, were they able, would themselves have procured the wherewithal for their needs? Wherefore, attach little credence to things often said concerning which are such dishes and which their nature and instead of vainly seeking appropriate dishes, discover the proper way and place for dining, as all foodstuffs and beverages are aphrodisiacal if they are appropriately consumed. Otherwise, even were you daily to consume the top of the milk *(cavo di latte)*, which is considered greatly stimulating, or the marrow of an Indian tiger, yet know not the way or place to partake of these, your appetite will remain meagre and ineffectual. Wherefore, put your mind to the things that follow and practise the same regularly for you shall greatly benefit thereby.

If your taste is for sweet-smelling and light pastries, delicious cakes and such like confectionery, take fancy flour and artfully knead it and fashion partridges and pigeons of pastry, or whatever other beast or fowl you please. Commit these to the oven and when they are well-baked, place them on your table and leave them to cool and sweeten. Then bare yourself entirely and call your lady to dine. Have her bare herself thoroughly in like manner and set her supine on the table. Next take the partridges and entrust them to her breasts, and in similar fashion set the pigeons upon her belly. If you have fashioned a cat or duckling or spring hare, take these pastries and place them upon her crotch that they may acquire lustre from the fragrance of her air. Then, select tasty morsels from wherever you may please, feed your lady incessantly and stoke her at will.

Candies and sweetmeats are likewise to be consumed on a naked and supine woman. When, therefore, your appetite is for women and sweetmeats, betake yourself to a confectioner's and provision yourself with pies and tarts, flans, meringues, marshmallows and eclairs and all forms of pastry and all the products of Arabian cacao and bring them all and spread them neatly over the folds and crevices of her body and lick them together with her fleshly parts.

Honeyed sweets and pastello are to be eaten on the vulva and fundament. Whereupon, having provisioned yourself with honey balls, nougat and fudge, together with puddings and smooth and delicious cream pies and a whole range of syrupy kadayif and baklava, take your lady with joy and delight and, having entered your bathroom with her and having performed your ablutions together, place her either prostrate or supine upon your couch and cover her every nook and cranny with the honeyed and syrupy fare. Thence, set to tasting the concoction with an appetite and you will feel yourself flowing with juices and your mouth watering insatiably. You may also avail yourself of her oven on the very spot, if you find it clean and fired. Yet chew slowly and calmly, not hastily or cursorily, and duly savour all the tastes and smells, the common and composite, the holy and unholy, since only thus will you be rendered both steward and partaker. And give praise to your Lord for such sustenance and beverage.

Fruits are always to be consumed in their season on a naked woman lying either in prone position or in reverse. Should you be eating apples and these are congenial to her and alike to her limbs, say to her "O that I, the apple-keeper, might savour you, my joyous and coveted Apple and never have my fill of you!" Or, if her delicate body reminds you of a delectable pear, say to her "O that I might savour you, my fresh and fragrant pear for I am unable to drain you dry, my sweet!" Fresh figs are to be consumed beside a succulent and mellifluous vulva. Break the fruit in two, see whether it conceals any canker within, and eat it skin and all. Dried figs are best eaten soaked in a lady's perfumed liquids either prior to coition or afterwards should you prefer.

Roasted chickpeas, chestnuts, walnuts, hazelnuts, almonds and nuts of all kinds are eaten upon a seated and naked woman. Cast them in plenty between the joints of her limbs that they may be impregnated, even into her dark inner recesses, and then take them one by one with your fingers and gracefully delight in them.

If you wont is for dishes that are oily, roasted or boiled, sit at your table like a civilised person and dine normally. Thereupon procure the desserts and proceed as above.

13.
Concerning Erotic Bussing and Veneration

As it appears also in treatises composed by the Greeks of old, the main manifestations of erotic bussing and carnal embraces are three: the earthy pre-coital, the moist coital and the airy post-coital, this latter also being known as post-veneration. Yet the forms and combinations of such embraces are numerous and hence difficult to commit to memory through study or practice. Wherefore, these men of old, distinguished by their deep wisdom and largesse yet also by their indomitable appetite for coition and interminable copulation, eventually discovered a method for classifying the forms of kissing in such a way that even the most maladroit in such matters might imprint them on his mind and apply them in his daily life.

Just as the Alexandrian Grammarians classified the seventeen consonants of the Greek tongue into three categories corresponding to their nature and sound, viz. mute, semivowels and double, so also the three main forms of kissing are the mute, semivowel and double forms. And just as the mute consonants are divided into labial, dental and palatal, so also the mute kisses are offered and accepted in labial, dental and palatal fashion. Similarly, just as the semivowel consonants are classified as nasal (m and n), liquid (l and r) and spirant (s), so also with the semivowel kisses: some have a nasal sound and are stifled within, others have a liquid sound and flow between the lips, while still others are spirant and coquettish. Finally, the double consonants (viz. sd, ks and ps) arise from a combination of mute and spirants. Hence the so-called double kisses arise when a deep hissing or sighing burst passes through the lips, teeth or palate.

Should you therefore wish to become a savant and master in this gentle art of bussing, apply yourself to the study of phonology and you shall greatly profit thereby.

Should your cohabitor be endowed with the gift of becoming fleshly and honeyed during the cohabitation and of emitting perfumed draughts and heady syrups, sample forthwith her lips' caresses, her tongue-play and her sucking, and nuzzle her from hairs to spittle and quaff her and drain her, though take care lest she inundate you. And proceed thus till the time comes for her well-spring to gush and blaze. And only then give thought to your verge (which all this time grazed alone in the hillocks and plains) and allow it to strike and flail your lady for the time that you are cajoling her and venerating her on bended knee. Upon consummation of your coition, instead of bussing and nuzzling her deductively, engage rather in kissing her additively; to wit, turn your tongue-play within her, especially if her vulva is still quivering and requires further conversation and placation.

Should your beloved have a propensity to release her fluids prior to coition so that you face the danger of finding yourself drowned in her river, do not give yourself to liquid kisses, viz. with an excess of l and r sounds, but do this same nasally and inhale her as those accustomed to snuff and as opium eaters inhale their substances through the nose. Whereupon, before penetrating into the fathomless depths of her vulva and encountering the streams of her fluids, cling first to her lips and avail yourself of a goodly dose of her liquids and thence bring your nose to the cleft of her hairs and, so doing, buss it till the fluids and liquids abate and grow stable. In similar cases, certain amorists are wont to have recourse to the so-called cycle of communicating vessels, whereby while having their verge in the lady's palatal vault and discharging joyfully, at the same time they imbibe her liquids either through the nose or the lips.

Amorous ladies who are in the habit of dissolving during the various steps of carnal intercourse and of ascending to the heights in a wondrous manner are best served by kisses that are purely palatal or palatal-like. Thus, when you see the lady copulating with you begin to gradually become rarefied like to a white cloud in the far reaches of the sky, be mindful that she is discarding her vital air and may well choke on you. Wherefore, while you are plying her and exploring her flesh, open her mouth as they do with those asphyxiated in rivers or wells and introduce the whole of your breath into her palate, during which time you will discharge and exhale your seed below. If the union is truly impassioned and your breath libidinous and gentle, her entire palate may open so as to resemble the dome of a church resounding during service or, yet more, a celestial dome covering the entire earth whether the sun shines and burns or whether it rains and snows.

Dental kisses are unbecoming for women who are pious or fasting. Therefore, employ dental kisses when copulating with idle and lethargic women, also known as lie-abeds. First peck the tiny lilies of their fingers and toes, then turn your attention to anything masticable they may possess (teats, ear lobes and concha, elbows, knees and ankles) and work your way to their lips and tongues, both upper and lower.

Should you crave within for the legendary kiss of the angels to the stars, yet are not angel-born, take up your lady, the same that excites and inflames you, and ascend with her on high, either on a mound, or on your rooftop, or on the top of your couch, and having made all the preparations for the sacrifice to love and for the rites, humble yourself, till you are raised to your highest pride, gently incense her image as it shines betwixt the divine images, and reverently perfume all her bodily limbs like a true servant of the Lord. Then cross yourself normally and place your lips upon her sacred lips (upper and lower) and insinuate your tongue into the freshness of hers and fall to the ground and venerate her as happens with holy and virginal divinities, with awe, faith and love. Remain thus for a sufficient length of time, the one sealed inside the other, and you will feel your bodies gradually ascending and hovering in the air with only their tongues bound fast.

14.
On How to Make
Erotic Music

If you are overly burdened by the garb of your solitude and your ears are assailed by the common confusion and din and you wish to ring light and blissful, betake yourself on an afternoon in July and sit beneath a stout and distant fig-tree. Discard your clothes and bathe yourself in a nearby stream, outwardly and inwardly. Then, lay yourself against the trunk of the tree and remain listening to the stillness of the hour, yet harken too to the Cicada's songs. When you are well relaxed and feel yourself suitably freshened, tune your instrument and string it that it may vibrate radiantly and insouciantly like to the leaves of the fig-tree. Then strike its chords *Doh Re Mi Fa* and you will hear your body's music echoing sweetly and all the noonday creatures, the wild beasts and wicked sprites, will gather beside you and, ecstatic and enchanted, will sit at your feet and will venerate you in their languor.

IF you are stoking a lady most demure yet also unmusical and taciturn, plant your verge laterally into the chords of her vulva and ply her in deep plagal mode, and straightway her ears will rejoice and she will sing for you most melodiously the hymns "Hail to Thee" and "How great is my Lord".

If you are stoking a woman both reverberant and fluidal and you wish to bring her into harmony with the sound of your verge thereby to create a most captivating duet, place your flute between vulva and duct and keep puffing. If your wish is for a rousing solo, place your verge in the canopy of her mouth and allow her to sing with you and play your pipe.

ALTERNATIVELY: Do as that most illustrious of Hellenes, Yoryis Karaiskakis, who aired his member in the face of the enemy and beat it in terrifying fashion either to the sound of the tambour or as a dümbelek.

15.
Introduction to Erotic Prosody

If you consider yourself sufficiently amorous and fervent yet take delight in prosody and rhythm, do as the Ancient Greeks (and Romans likewise), who, being truly amorous and most musical, gave stress and rhythm to all their deeds and acts of coition, aware that by nature an ordinate movement is more congenial than an inordinate one.

The most rapid rhythm is the trochee, for which reason it is adjudged more improprietous than the rest. Wherefore, if you are mounted upon your lady (paramour or spouse) and are in haste, stoke her in trochee mode, viz. first long then short ($-\cup$). Once you have mastered the simple trochaic foot from the fore, reverse your Poetess and come at her from the rear with double trochees, viz. strike twice long and twice short simultaneously. When the double feet are smooth, form your verses longer still in trochaic tetrameter and hold the rhythm steady with no regard for hiatus or caesura.

The iamb is most like to speech and commonplace. Wherefore, if you dispose of time and leisure, stoke your lady in iambic mode, viz. commence with a short and end with a long ($\cup-$), no matter whether your composition is metrical or stress-timed. Thus, when you have fashioned numerous iambs and your couch is ringing most musically, bring yourself to the accustomed metre of the dramatists and stress everything staccato in iambic trimeters. If your preference is for dialogic coitus, viz. opposite and face to face, keep your trimeters acatalectic. In cases of many actors, during a tragic contest, take pains neither to ignore the zeugmata or enjambments or the basic diaereses.

Know that the dactylic hexameter is the verse of epic, heroic and also didactic poetry. If therefore you wish to commence the teaching of verse, begin with the dactyl, viz. show your fair pupil a long syllable in the first beat and two short ones in the following ($-\cup\cup$). Take not as your example the verse "Sing, goddess, of the wrath of Peleus' son Achilles", which presents difficulty on account of the shortened hiatus, but show her the verse "Tell me, Muse, of the man of many turns, who travelled many ways", which is more regular and reveals many things indeed. That the metre may be varied, do not overlook the diaereses, particularly the bucolic, and avoid wholly dactylic or spondaic verses.

If it pleases you to copulate in a standing position, the best metre by far is the anapest, which begins with two short feet and ends with a long one ot equal duration (∪∪–). Verses composed in anapests are lengthy and grave, yet soon cause fatigue. Hence, commence anapestic stoking during your entrance, holding your dancing partner by the buttocks, and on completion of two rounds, return to iambs or trochees.

For such as are fond of the rhythmic but not of full prosody, the most fitting rhythms are the paeon or else the Kretan melody. Yet as is remarked by those versed in such matters, this rhythm should be combined with the rest, else it becomes heavy and wanes. Thus, after having lubricated and attuned yourself thoroughly and unfailingly, commence your stoking with the first paeon, viz. with one long syllable and three successive short ones (–∪∪∪). Thereafter, when you have had your fill of a variety of rhythms and metres, end by discharging your seed with the fourth paeon, viz. strike three successive short syllables and an extended long one (∪∪∪–).

16.
Concerning Words that One Should Say During Coition

In the same way that women vary in the kind and con-formation of their vulva, so also do they differ in their coition and in like manner the fair words befitting them on each occasion also change. Wherefore, be mindful of the circumstance and act accordingly.

Should it be your fortune to mount a horsy lady with ample croup and your desire is for a long ride, yet without in any way becoming weary or limp from the abundance of flesh, assume the position of the Uru beast, that both stokes and nuzzles at once. Thus, come upon the hollow of her lower vulva, or the folds of her ears, or the bridle of her teeth, saying to her in plain English and distinctly: "O that I may sow you, my Unploughed one, and that not a seed be lost. O that I may plough your stony ground that it may flourish. Lean now to the left, my Poseuse, for my ploughshare is turning awry. Now bend to the right to aid me, my Citrus. Now stoop to face the plain and sustain your ardour for I have planted myself with my head below. I poke and I stoke and I stoke and I poke, shaking all over, o seed!" And thereupon she will quiver to the roots of her flesh and submissively will fashion for you the furrows one by one and you will avail yourself most cheerily of them for four hours of the clock.

Should you be serving a cat-like and furtive lady, keep your tongue closed to plain words, so as not to unhinge the coup-ling and topple over, and prefer parable and ambiguity. Wherefore, instead of saying: "O that I may flow everlastingly in your rivulets, my Lily White, O that I may leap quivering upon your tiny stones and lacerate myself," say "your fair flesh is my bounty, O my beloved, till I have hewn out your airy caverns. O that I may espy you on the edge of my couch and engulf you entire! Thresh your briny liquids that I may drown in you, my Merciless. Behold me, impoverished as I am! Shake your plump little limbs, for on account of your currents I expire, my wild, my Willing." Or constantly repeat to her the Curse of the Black Mountain "O that your Mount may tremble, Hellcat, and that the fingers of the Scorched may stand upon it." Speak thus to her and take care for fear of overturning and study her assiduously *ala recto* and *ala verso* that you may come to know her deeply.

Should, anon, your wish be to copulate with a hare-like and timid lady, address her to her face and most openly, for beings of such kind like brashness and boldness though feign the opposite. Whereupon, as you ride and grow wet inside her lard, say to her "Now I have you and rejoice in you, my Vanity, for your part climb down and lap us both. Come then, my Desire, reveal to me the slit unmade by hand. What care you, my Fair? I shall enter and retire and it shall still be yours. O how I love to insert my flute and play it for you, my teat. Place your tiny ears upon your navel and bring your buttocks high over your shoulders and open, my Housemaid, that I my sweep you, croup and all." Or say to her "I shall clasp your flesh entire and you shall consume me." And she will warm to you and will straightway unsaddle.

Should you be stoking a woman at once spidery and fanciful and your wish is for peace and gratification, speak to her as brother to sister, that she may regard you as her own and as familiar. Wherefore say to her "O gentle sister of my flesh, regard how the seed and blood that bore us is one and the same. How lovely is my Sister, of one fluid! Let us mingle our blood in the common Womb. Regard my nipple that you may suckle and leave me to drink from your teats. Plant your incestuous kiss upon me and I shall languor beneath your bodice. O my sister's slender breasts! Assist me that we may bring together what has been set apart, O my mouth's fragrance and saliva". This and more will you say to her and, ever alert, you will await and should you see her drowsy, open her blackest recesses and whiten them frenziedly and arduously, like to the infant that with gulps of milk in his mouth yet cries for his mother and gobbles all up.

Should you find yourself upon a woman who is dove-like and deceptive and you risk wilting because of the fickleness of her being, reveal to her with not a little tact that you are infirm for you are in want of a children's ditty, now forgotten in your tongue. Whereupon, request that she sing it to you in her own manner that you may recover. And when she begins to sing "Ah my Dear and Ah Mother mine and envied Bird in foreign parts," pronounce the words with her and hum the tone and melody. And if she says "Aah, and take me in the wood, my Sweet", do you the same "Aah" and string it out. And if she says "Yo and heave ho and I am all awash," then you heave likewise to the "Yo" and "Ho" of the seafarer. Yet should she refuse to sing for you and your craving grows worse, then take out a black kerchief to mop the sweat from your brow, sound the horn with "Woe, Woe and Thrice Woe" and crow as the cock whose throat is slashed.

All the aforementioned I took and recorded from a Persian treatise, translated for my needs from Farsi into the Roumi tongue.

17.
On How Your Member May Be Unceasingly and Consummately Erect

Should for your needs you desire an erection like the olive tree, viz. unyielding, then proceed as follows. Slay a black cockerel, red-crested, having previously had it consecrated and kept celibate for a score of days. Collect the fowl's blood in a pewter bowl, taking pains not to spill as much as one drop, and while thus engaged, recite this incantation: "As your blood spatters and frolics, so may my seed spatter and frolic." Then take hold of the still warm fowl and place it unplucked upon a white faïence platter and open up its intestines till you are gripped by it and full of feeling. Shore off the fowl's sweetbreads and place them jointly in the bowl of blood. Thereupon, bare the wrist of your left hand (since, as you have surely observed, at the commencement of erection, the member flutters slightly to the left) and inscribe upon it the sign of the Holy Cross. Take a needle from a woman betrothed and pure of menses and prick the cross till it drips seven drops of blood, mixing this with the blood of the fowl. Cast into the pewter bowl two pinches of powdered cantharides, three pinches of Ceylon powder and ten grains of salified salts. Take a ladle and stir the mixture while chanting to yourself the hymn to the saint whose name you bear or to whom you have been pledged. When the mixture has thickened, carefully carry out your ablutions both without and within, perfume yourself, and call sensuously to whichever paramour most inflames you and entreat her to lap your privates grain by grain that the vulnerableness of your sex may be washed away. And once she has lubricated you most thoroughly and most nakedly, take the mixture and apply it to genitals, kidneys and heart every three hours of the clock.

Do this most frequently, nocturnally, at the moon's waxing, never during its waning, for as long as seven months, and you will be hale for ever more. It is said that in order to attain a better erection, men in the land of Italy sing a ballad with each new month, which, should you so wish, you may commit to memory: "O fortuna, velut luna, semper variabilis, aut crescis, nunc decrescis". Sometimes they sing this playing guitars, sometimes to the accompaniment of the mandolin or celesta.

ALTERNATIVELY: Procure the dried seeds of the Arabian tree which the local inhabitants call Pausintelia Yohimbana – though which in the Grecian tongue is known as the sensuous iochimbina. Grind these in a galvanised mortar for three whole nights following the first day of the month. If you are a man of cool temperament, add juice of trachum (herba artificiosa), most delectable, digestible, fragrant and productive of sperm. If you are phlegmatic by temperament, add the juice of finocchio (foeniculum), which opens the eyes, whence its name, for it renders sight even to vipers. These same hide in their nests and holes all winter long and on emerging in summer are as though blind and regain their sight by rubbing their eyes on the finocchio. Wherefore, this mixture helps in opening your lower eyes and allows your tool to venture forth with fine ocular powers. If you are prone to rancour, keep clear of finocchio for it provokes great ardour and you risk bloating, which is in no way aphrodisiacal. Many are they who add ox-tongue or poppy, which renders great comfort to the veins. Quickly swallow the beverage morn and night after first having your glans amply lubricated by either paramour or spouse and you shall reap great profit therefrom.

ALTERNATIVELY and at no cost: Take a red cotton thread, as used for candle wicks. Stand most erect and thoroughly perform your ablutions. Take hold of the fine thread and immerse it in oil of tahina or curds and wind it around your member, starting from the root, yet leave the glans free for tongue-play, whether this be in thought or deed. Stand facing East and open yourself to the sun, till you are thoroughly warm, and clearly recite the incantation of the famished, viz. of the hungering. Thereupon (insofar as you are thoroughly cleansed), you will observe your member shaking from the roots and growing right robust and vigorous that all the threads snap. This is most easily done by those who know well

the song of the famished and the erection may last uninter-
ruptedly for three whole days. Yet for the uninitiated, it is
dangerous and conducive to phimosis. For which reason, take
care to do it diligently and most reverently.

18.
On How to Discharge
Your Seed at Will

Take hellebore, white and black, three hermodactyls (iris tuberosa), essence of amaranthus sempervivum, next obtain fresh honey roasted in the May sun, Judaean stones, viz. lapis Judaecus, four ounces of which, and two grains of musk. Place all the aforementioned in a pot and commit it to a fiery oven for five hours of the clock. When this mixture has thickened and cooled, take two spoonfuls of the same and apply it to your verge (having previously washed this most thoroughly). After two hours you will feel yourself overflowing with your nature's aerial and fluidal semen and with all as moves within your body.

Thereupon, betake yourself to the paramour who least impassions and enchants you and lay her bare as when she was born. While you are copulating with her from the rear and her breasts are beating with the movement, insert one of your fingers in the mixture and offer it to her to suckle insatiably. The moment you see the finger being consumed and about to vanish, allow your seed to be discharged resonantly through the canal of your verge and say: "Lord, just as five thousand souls were gladdened by five loaves and three fishes, so let many fair ladies be gladdened by this my solitary and homeless Orphan" and discharge yourself most consummately. Thereupon, rise, wash, take the mixture and betake yourself to another paramour higher in the order of ardour and enchantment. Do as above and once again you will discharge most satisfactorily and profusely.

When you have thus passed cheerily and refreshingly through all the paramours in due order yet happen to be wedded and legally bound, rub your entire body with the remaining mixture, enter your chamber in all modesty and say to your lady: "So many channels have I passed through, my pride and joy, and I have filled them all, yet still I am overflowing. Behold, here I am before you and my strongest seed I have kept for you, my lovely and my last." And when she says

113

to you: "O, my lord, do as you desire and are able", and bends low, as you mount and spur her, offer her all the fingers that she may suckle, and delve within yourself and release dawn's black and wattled cockerel and, crowing ten times, discharge your seed at will and to your greater glory.

19.
How to Render a Vulva Moist till it Overflow Mysteriously

Since a woman's vulva is by its nature mysterious, furtive and cavernous, sometimes enveloping you in all its moistness till it swamps you in its channel and sometimes holding you exceedingly dry and parched, as in a desert, proceed, therefore, as follows and you shall forever find delight just as the eel rejoices in the flowing streams and the birds of the air in the hills.

Lay bare the lady most thoroughly and with each garment that you remove from her, quietly murmur the hymn of tailoring and the song of the needle and the ode to the silk chemise which for seven long days they fashioned yet it was never finished. Once you have unclothed her and sung to her as is befitting, cross her from top to bottom and from her midriff to her rib-bones to rid her of the tight air of garments and straps. Thereupon, instruct her to arrange herself for you either supine and wide-open or prostrate and closed and lubricate her fully and reverently and, anon (after two hours), insert your finger within her mouth and take her spittle and lap it with relish. Likewise, insert your finger between your lips and give her to drink deeply thereof that your liquids may become alike, that which the ancients called commutation.

When the liquids of the upper founts emerge and multiply and flood the divine aspects of your mouths, render lips, tongue and teeth as one morsel and feed her with consonants and vowels and your own self with hers. Thence, when you see that the upper level of her liquids has settled and the excess is flowing from the cracks in her lips, once again take her finger and place it in the canal of your verge which is also known as the fount of the living water and vein of the seminal word and moisten her finger and take it with due awe and reverence and place it on her inner key, lubricating it most meticulously. Do this twice and thrice and oftentimes till her organ's key begins to glow and her juices overflow down into her rivulet and her rushes drink deeply and grow verdant.

And when the rivulet is filled and gently foams, then let your cockerel float and crow, as ducklings and water fowl flow in the reeds, and let the wet wind pass through the reeds that they may be infused by the azure song of the languorous. Then you will see your lady swoon and quiver and from afar you will hear her flow outpouring and her liquids gushing, and before you, for your part, can move but twice or thrice, lo, her heavenly firmament will open and her mysterious liquids will flow in abundance and will render the earthy aqueous and will unite the land with the sea. And you, reverent and versed as you are, will assume the position of the diver of a thousand fathoms and will surrender yourself headfirst to the foam and will plunge therein. Then, as you arise most slowly from her depths (also known as Adam's deep), open your eyes wide to the breeze and you will observe the waters again becoming calm as she abates and returning hastily to their founts. And her entire land from one end to the other will again shine most brightly and the sun will again emerge fully in her firmament for her fleshly world has lately been born and revealed.

20.
On How to Ward Off the Evil Eye when Comely and Fair in Limb

If you are indeed fair in limb and male by nature, yet susceptible to the evil eye, keep next to your flesh a sprig of angelweed. Just as this in no way withers, so you too will remain unwilting. Equally, have hanging around your neck a stone of emerald, which lends power both amorous and aversive. Thus you will entice and bewitch, yet be neither bewitched nor enfeebled. Yet most wondrous of all is this which follows: betake yourself to volcanic places and seek rock as yet uncooled, viz. soft and malleable, and fashion your figure most faithfully and naked in limb. Be sure, however, that your privates and pudenda acquire the colour of aqua mare, which glows at night and is clearly discernible. Set your image in a window facing south and let abundant light fall upon your limbs. Should some male pass by and admire you, then he will take upon himself the malediction. Should it be a woman and she covets you, allow her to savour you as in dreaming, till she be sated and swoon. Thus be wary regarding ardent paramours and sweethearts. Should these come to you impassioned and unclad, straightway cast down your image and smash it. For thus their hold will be broken and you will remain unharmed.

ALTERNATIVELY: If you are comely and amorous and are burdened by the gazes of others and enfeebled, then in order to avoid the mischief, engage in frenzied rummaging (or stoke yourself unrestrainedly) till you grow wan and wither by your own hand.

If you are (or appear) a lady truly fair and womanly, and are beset by many eyes and thereby lose your glow, keep bound between your breasts a stone like to a chestnut which has within it another smaller one and which rattles like the almond nut. The same stone which the Italians call aquiline and the Hellenes eaglestone. For thus, the stone will absorb the perturbation and you no more than the puzzlement and wonder. Yet, when you are about to retire to bed and disrobe, be sure to place the stone upon the labia of your vulva that this may fall silent in sleep and night's eyes may not harm you.

ALTERNATIVELY for most womanly ladies: Don your finest dress and wear no other article of clothing upon you. Betake yourself at some midday hour to the square frequented by the virile and voracious, and when, anon, you see these same piercing you and fixing you with their gazes, discard your dress without ado and shine stark naked before them that they may be blinded by the glare. Do as the Lord on the Mount of the Transfiguration, when He revealed Himself in His glory and blinded the irreverent. Be sure to do this four days following your menses, since then your liquids flow fragrant and your inner glow acquires flesh. Should you be coveted by women and these same cast the evil eye upon you when approaching your couch (in dream or actuality), betake yourself, naked and proud, to your garden at night time. Assume there the pathetic mien of the angel-struck and rest your head in your hands innocently and reflectively. When, anon, the moon appears and pours itself upon the earth's verdure, recite the hymn of Amat: straightway you will be granted his halo and the evil and malediction will vanish. Thereafter, you may now be venerated without fear or risk by your tribades and paramours and, as they lubricate you reverently, they will name you the Lady of Succour and Sweetness.

21.
On How to Dream of a Lady Whom you Loved yet never Possessed

Avail yourself of and give heartfelt praise to your solitude, since the fleshliness of your dreams seeks the solitary and ethereal. Prepare your couch upon an open veranda, facing south, that you may clearly survey all the constellations in the firmament, the commonplace Pleiades together with the radiant Alektor. Betake yourself to bed at the eleventh hour or thereabouts, having previously sprinkled your pillow with five or six droplets of aromatic liquid known as the tears of Christ (lacrimae Christi), for He too loved yet possessed not. Whereupon, see to it that you sleep undisturbed and soundly for at least four hours.

When four hours have thus passed, move slightly and assume the position of the embryo in the belly, viz. place your right hand as your pillow and draw up your legs like wings enfolded. Thereafter, reflect, though sleeping still, on all that you possessed and lost, all you possess and are losing, not so to grieve, but on the vanity of it. Whereupon, once you feel a rush of tears sweeping you out to sea, take from within you a musical instrument, no matter whether lute, mandolin or drum, and strike up most passionately and rhythmically as in a dream. And set the melodious paths of the verses that become you all around indiscriminately as garlands to safeguard you, yet neglect not the melodious path of Lethe and play this unfailingly twice and thrice. Whereat, shining before you will appear trails of dreams, some black as pitch, some of reddish hue and others the colour of saffron. Without more ado yet with no little awe, take the one dream path that leads you to your heart's desire and follow it with utmost care for at least fifty miles. For here is the place that deep in the night you will find her sitting all alone upon a rock, or in her master's dwelling, or wedded to another and busy with her household and content.

Then come up to her most softly that she may not awaken and be alarmed and call to her within you, as only you know,

O Irene, O Lucy, O Elspeth, O Christina. And, if she still hearkens and feels for you, she will turn towards you, as in dreaming, and you will say to her in the Romaic tongue, "Regard how because of you I am alone and my tears rejoice in you, for you have gladdened me this night, my Sweetest." Say to her no more than this since it is not expedient, given that time is pressing, but turn back once more and make your return. Yet should she not hearken to you when you address her and no longer feel for you on account of the length apart, do not be embittered or grieve overly much, for you were worthy of her shade and image. Whereupon, collect yourself and seek another more amenable.

If you would employ dreams in such a manner, take care not to exceed two or three each year. The most propitious time is August, on the sixth day, the feast of the first fruits and our Saviour's Transfiguration, or on the morrow of the Assumption, feast of the Holy Shroud, unless, that is, this falls on Sunday. Otherwise, do this in August, on the twenty-ninth day, feast of the Precursor's Beheading.

22.
On How to Possess a Woman in Dream

If you are oft visited by the dream of a woman who is at once hazy and insubstantial and who at times flutters around you like a creature of the air and at others swims around you like one of the sea so that you are unable to grasp her, know that this is because your desire for her is likewise hazy and insubstantial. Wherefore, should you wish to savour her in flesh and wholly naked, meditate upon either the lone hunter or the sleepless fisherman and catch her as follows. First instruct yourself in the path of her habits and follow her in dream for no less than thirty days in succession and let neither the stream of her air nor the wisp of her fragrance escape you. When you are fully versed in all her currents and the secret pathways to which her limbs turn to find sustenance and her thoughts to find refreshment, choose a night most dark and give yourself to slumber for three hours of the clock.

When this fanciful creature comes to you in dream and you espy your reverie approaching you as a bird flittering all about you in the hills of fantasy, take the dregs of aged wine and mix these well with wheat or other cereals and scatter this same over the place where she is wont to walk. Thereafter, betake yourself to the same place and when you see her eating of the grains and becoming inebriate, speak to her as you wish and say to her "O the one vision of my life, nocturnal and hapless. Regard how I sit at your marble window that I may gaze upon you, my Jewel and my Gem, who ever fades and vanishes before me so that my arms are left ever clutching at the darkness. Come, my Truest, disperse my dream's haze and discard your flimsiness." Straightway, she will unfold her wings and fly to you in her inebriety, yet also in her amorousness. Whereupon, reach out through the dream's window and grasp her most gently by her plumage and draw her within to where you are sitting and gazing and put her to your breast that she may take heart.

When, anon, four hours have elapsed and the cockerels

of the earth awaken you, you will see her in all truth sitting upon your couch in her fleshliness and nakedness. Whereupon, she now being the possession and discovery of your dreams, nuzzle her most diligently and lubricate her feathers, beaks and tongues and rummage her in the way and the magnificence of the swan that mounts and closes with a woman.

If again she comes to you in dream and you see her floating on the breeze like a fish in the sea and you feel her black waters washing over and drowning you, fashion forthwith a lantern of glass or crystal, in such a way that the water cannot enter and render its base of wood and watertight. Keep it tightly sealed and place within it a candle or wick, attaching lead that it may sink but not be snuffed. And let it have a ring that you may tie it and lower it into the sea. Once you see a myriad of womanly forms swarming around the light, take up your net and land the one that stings you most with her scales and barbs and assails you with her tail, saying to her "O my white waters and mermaid sea. I am unable to cross you for I ever sink and swallow brine. Leave the sea's waves and the murky depths behind and I shall await you on the water's surface. For I am mortal, my Slippery one, and am drowning." Then she will arise from the sea like a mysterious luminescence and thrice she will ask you the same question. And likewise you will answer thrice and awaken. And upon waking, you will see her naked and wet, writhing at your side, just as a real woman. Grasp her then by the tail and open her in womanly fashion and as you stoke her, buffeted and dizzy as you are from the pounding of her waves, take hold of her breasts and her breasts' nipples and imbibe the milk of the sister of one who in olden times was called Alexander.

23.
On How to Delight in Men and Women through Olfaction

S hould you be possessed by a male love and your wish is to most fully delight in him through smell and touch, come upon him when insouciant and inexpectant and proceed as follows: ply him with blandishments and first wash him well and in womanly fashion either in a bath or spa. Then lay him naked as his mother bore him, lubricate him most meticulously for protection and for a shiny appearance and set him to sleep for four hours of the clock. Thereupon, bare yourself thoroughly and stand beside his pillow without sleep or pride. Have with you a phial of Venetian glass and place inside this three leaves of Kretan Lovewort (dictamus cretensis), three sprigs of hyssop and a root of human shape, thus named mandrake (mandragora officinarum). Sprinkle seven droplets of olio d'amore, three teardrops from your inner inconsolable eyes and two dashes of your libidinous humours. When the first hour has passed and you see his body breathing with virility, approach and smear the mixture evenly either upon his mouth, or lips, or head, though do not yet turn to the breast for it is there that dreams are woven and you may well provoke them.

Move downwards to his breast at the second hour, slowly lubricating him with your tongue, and fashion a wet pentacle on his belly and sprinkle two droplets from the phial into his navel. Then place him lovingly upon his sheet, just as gentle Joseph received the body of Christ into his hands. When some time has elapsed and the diaphragm has fully imbibed the mixture, move towards his genitals, just as the viper slithers in the dry leaves unheard. Thereupon, take spittle together with love's humours and anoint him thoroughly, with tongue and touch, and taking your droplets, daub him to the very soles of his feet, fore and aft. Then, at around the third hour, open up your gills like the fish that writhes and deeply smell the love that rankles you. Forthwith you will see how your insides overflow with libidinous smells as his body pours out the

133

springtime of the men known as Crags and Mariners and Winds and you will be seduced by the scents and will pour into the firmament like the fumes from sacred incense. From that very same moment you will possess him and he will be yours forever.

Know also that should you wish to smell a woman to her very foundation and your innards yearn at her very name, you may inhale her imprudently like smoke so that she vanishes inside you. Wherefore, before you essay this, thrice perfume her with spikehard, unbeknown to her, and pronounce the words of the Solomonic spell: "*In lama safra sa ima, dare corpa lama na ita*", viz. "To the air I air you, so surrender to me, air." When, anon, you see her ready to swoon, clasp her, warm as she is, and bare her to her inmost parts. Take a sea sponge and first wash her body with distilled kindi tsitseyi root so to lighten it and then rub it with chrysochorton, viz. golden herbage, that it may shine. Set her to rest for seven hours and seat yourself beside her, thoroughly naked, and admire her, yet take care lest you cast the evil eye upon her. When you sense her tiny heart beginning to flutter, lean over her and lightly smell all her hirsute parts, viz. hair, eyebrows, eyelashes, armpits and genitals. Leave for last the freshness of her upper lip and imbibe not of this that she may have it as her charm and protection.

When, anon, you have had your fill of the air of her every hair and you are enmeshed in your intoxication, take a silver cup or a thimble of gold and fill it with your teardrops, for thus it will be seen that you are worthy of the spiritual smells. Should you be unable to weep and remain dry, leave the woman in peace and retire for the undertaking is not a little dangerous. If you weep desirously, gather up your tears and sprinkle them from your cup into her body's nine orifices. And each time smell this same deeply, in the ears, the nostrils, the eyes and the mouth. Should you be short of teardrops for the eighth and ninth orifice, despair not, for here you may sprinkle libidinous humours in place of tears. Wherefore, passionately seize your slumbering one and, taking hold of her eighth orifice, gently open it in its length, breadth and depth. And if her liquids trickle into the leaves, lick them, and if they pour into the roots, take root and smell them for no less than two hours of the clock. At the third hour, come upon the ninth orifice and say, *Acouel, eisbel, dor, vinerian, camenanton, ektilen, ekpilen, briskadedeos, dedessa, paga, thy sophasodotion*, and straightway this will be unloosed and you will smell her to her foundation and she shall remain consummately yours for you have inhaled her most secretly. Thereupon, when you have sated your nasal olfaction, allow your verge to smell her and stoke the woman cheerily for three full hours, saying "As I delight in you now, my Booty, so may I take you my Beauty." Then gather yourself in and allow her to wake sans souci.

24.
On How to Make an Unyielding Lady Grow Weak at Your Very Name

If you are inflamed by a woman at once elusive and intract-able yet this same snubs you with exceeding stubbornness and scorn, proceed as follows: obtain the membrane of an unborn beast and wash it in water seven times, clean it and fashion from it unbegotten paper, saying to yourself *Olaï, Iaou, Maroukata, Adonaïs, Semporphyry, la, la, o Tetragram and Sophar, sacred, awesome and frightful name, cleanse the uncleanliness of this beast and bind fast all that I inscribe, world without end.* Then bring holy water and sprinkle it thrice upon the skin and take a quill and boldly inscribe the name of your unyielding one, thrice and in serpentine fashion. At the first full-moon, place the paper upon you and betake yourself to her house, circling it nine times and holding her inside you like a painting yet thoroughly naked and uncovered.

At the ninth time recite the hymn of the famished, viz. of the hungering, and halt before her window and knock thrice. Thereupon, she will emerge, gentle and joyous, and she will call you by your name and say to you "Come my Stay and Saffron and Stalk." Enter prudently thereat and take her bodice and smell its air till it be empty. Next grasp her linen, saying "As you have trembled upon her, so let her tremble" and seize her and possess her in her fleshliness and lubricate her till she reddens and surrenders to her liquids. At the very moment that she is ready to heave her sigh, take out your kerchief and bring it to her mouth's orifice and catch the sigh and bind it with a double knot. And when she becomes fren-zied from the sorcery, bring your verge and let it roam her pathways and leave no corner unexplored for at least two hours. Yet neither ram nor stoke her, simply dress and retire just as you came, alone.

Allow four days to pass and, on the fifth, if you espy her fluttering at you proudly from afar, show to her the kerchief with the bound sigh and demand her favour. Whereupon, she will straightway loosen and grow weak and will fall before

139

you in obeisance and will open herself to you *ala gatto* and *ala cane* and she will squirm upon you like a black bitch in heat. Take her then and rummage her as you will and grapple her as you wish. And should you desire to couple with her in the street, demand it of her and so it shall be, and should you wish to mount her in the public square, do so without hesitation and keep her thus bound to your bidding and behest for a full five years. Then tear up the paper and grant her remission.

If the unyielding and obstinate lady be your wedded wife, do exactly as aforementioned, but in place of the hymn of the famished, recite the prayer *Glory be to the Father, the Son and the Holy Spirit*, and hum to her the "Wedding march". Straightway you will have her as your slave and servant and bitch, for as long as you wish and are able.

25.
On How to Spellbind Your Rival

If you are burning with fervent love for a wedded woman and wish to make her tire of her spouse and succumb to you *molto volontieri* and have her for yourself and for your own, take red silk and whitened hemp and black thread and join these, saying "As the sun and moon and stars in the heavens and the reds and whites and blacks of the airy spirits are bound fast, so too may this woman's man be bound. Thus do I bind the nerves in his knees and his regal vein that carries his sin into her fair body that it may be unable to move. I bind him from head to toe and from east to west, I bind his 12 veins and his 365 joints, I bind his seven vertebrae hand and foot and the vein of his erection and as for his shaft that he drives in and out of her fair body, may this too be bound and grow cold and droop, abject and ridiculous, as long as I so wish it and it please me, now and forever, world without end amen." Do this on the fifteenth day of the moon's cycle, unless this falls on Friday or Sunday, and you shall reap great benefit thereby.

ALTERNATIVELY: Betake yourself at break of day to the couple's domicile so to avert any impending coition or copulation and, having primed your tool in the open air, recite the following, *I clasp my untamed leash, I clasp my strings, I clasp my staff of cane, I journey to the mountains and the waters of the sea and to the sundered wind, o my tamed Wilder and Wont, thereby to find the devil. O silence of the crone, o bleating of the dotard, o smell of woman's blood, mountain of Zavoukles, shards of verge and wings of paper, o thus do I bind you. Loving and harmonious couple, I spit thus, mus, nach, nach, de, bb, le, le, kb, ry, ry, ver, rb the Great, rg the Blood, rd the Horrid, sal the alcana and stisiriou. I bind him and tighten, o demon, the bond. As nature is bound by the seasons so may I bind you, I bind your wits, I bind your back, may you go forth a man, return a cunnuch, may it growl yet not spurt, may it hate and detest the couch, orifice, channel and duct. May it droop and never rise. Behind Christ and before the devil Garazael, I bind him, amen."* Or else, take yourself in hand and discharge thrice into a reed pipe, planting this same at their door and within three days you will have her thoroughly naked, open and soiled by her liquids on your account.

26.
On How to Find Release from a Rival's Spell

Should you retire to bed with your wedded wife and are unable to rise due to the spell of some cunning and fiendish act, and are most shamed by your inactivity, take unbegotten paper and write "*Let heaven rejoice and earth delight. O you who have relieved the pains of the fettered and released their bonds, release me from my present infirmity, amen.*" Then take a knife previously used to commit a foul murder and bare the blade and place it between your legs, saying "As this same was raised and cut through flesh and drew blood and withdrew, gleaming, so too may I become and turn to steel. So may I insert myself entire and entire withdraw, may I enter parched and exit quenched. Jesu was crucified, Jesu was nailed, Jesu died and was resurrected and broke all bonds. Thus Kyrie Jesu, thrice-natured, thrice-blessed, thrice-membered, release my trident and my triad."

Thereupon, seize your spouse and bare her to her inner depths and set her kneeling full naked upon the floor. Then lower her head to the ground and raise her fair body upwards and, grasping her buttocks, open these wide and smell them in all their glory, and having thrice made the sign of the cross over her, chant to her "*I behold your bridal chamber adorned yet garb I have none to enter within.*" And as you see your verge begin to venture boldly forth, straightway lubricate her and rummage her to her very roots. And while you are rummaging and nuzzling, have with you a red crayon and inscribe upon her back this hymn *rtspactfl* (viz. release the spells and cool the flame) and sing praise to your Lord that your eyes beheld your redemption and thus you will remain released forever and unhindered in all your desires and passions.

27.
Erotic Anathemas and Imprecations

If you have been forsaken by a heavenly woman with a vulva both moist and redolent, in which it was your wont to plunge headfirst, as the illustrious diver that you are, and to emerge freshly bathed at the other side of the channel, anathematize and curse her as follows: "O that all your liquids may run dry, in fount and fundament, and that you may become arid like the Black Salt Desert whose cracks know no dew and through which not even a scent of earthly or heavenly water passes, so too may you crack open like a carapace. And may you be stoked by three at once and rammed fore and aft, from head to toe, while you remain sapless, and may your mouth be stopped by three wet and fleshly members and may your spittle drip upon them and, boiling, sizzle and evaporate like dewdrops upon a fiery iron anvil."

If formerly you enjoyed the care of a motherly woman who hugged you like an infant and gave you milk from her breast and swaddled you in the wrappings of her thighs, rocking you thereafter in the cradle of her crevice, yet this same deserted you for another, leaving you alone, hungry and sleepless, aye well, anathematize her thrice before the magnificence of Dawn and thrice again before the lowliness of Dusk, saying "A curse be upon you in the horror below and the filth above, Amen. May you be cast out of the Legion of amorous childbearers and may you wander as a wicked stepmother, and may your milk turn black, like your tears, and may your body's flesh be defiled and may your arms open to the sons of your bed and the daughters of your milk and may your armpits sprout thistles and thorns and may your vulva be rent asunder and may the seed and saliva of coition turn from you and may thick bushes grow in your channels and smother you as the rose is smothered by weeds and the woodland scrub."

If yours was a woman well versed in coition, yet avaricious and niggardly, and who, for another's riches and wares, cast you into orphanhood and penury, first curse her as far back as three generations of her lineage and imprecate her starting from her family's seed, blood and milk. Thereupon, take the black stone of simony and maliciousness and anathematize her, saying "A curse be upon you! Where once you were rich in the finery and adornments of my worship, may you now be impoverished to your last hair and thread. And may the wind be stopped from your nostrils, you who had my heaven's three score winds in the power of your breath, and may the saliva dry on your lips and brine and thirst's blisters cover your tongue, which you once lavishly sank in my humours and, while mounted by me, you whinnied, and may you inhale and choke and may your palate be devoid of moisture save for your steaming piss and may you discharge this and drink it alone with cupped hands, you who drew night and day on my sperm and rejoiced, and may you find not one leaf to shade you as my foliage shaded you in your heated ardour, and should one be found, may it be dry and bitter, Bitch, Black Hag."

28.
Concerning Remedies
for Sleeplessness

If you happen to be inflamed by an incurable love that forever holds you sleepless, solitary and sick at heart and you are unable on account of its obstinacy and whims to delight in it, body and flesh, yet this same encompasses you without compassion in a phantasm of grief and loneliness, proceed as follows and you will find respite and abundant pleasure to boot.

If your love is male in nature and unyielding and subjects you to everlasting sleeplessness and perturbation though he himself sleeps blissfully and shamelessly, secretly obtain from him either a kerchief or a vest or some other of his bodily garments, one that has been worn and has his odour, and await the new month of Spring and the darkest hour. Discard all your own garments (the outer and inner ones of your nature) and bathe and perfume yourself befittingly and, placing his garment upon your flesh, approach the window where to no avail you spend your sleepless nights. Thereupon, remove the garment from upon you and ritually wave it in the wind and there inscribe notionally and with due care to spelling "Yesual, Enaou, Avertaeton: O spirit and demon and aerial sprite: hearken to me and hear, shade of Spring, my beloved my Bel: begone and find for me this garment's owner, one who is perfumed and itinerant, and subdue for me this infidel, undefiled, idle and slumbering as he is. And wheresoever this same dwells, betake yourself thereto and bring him to the place where I sit and wait throughout the midnight hours. Let it so be for I have invoked you and now you are in my grip."

As you are notionally inscribing this, gently shake the garment in the wind and at once take incensed wax and fashion a puppy dog and call it by the name of he who rankles you. Next, place the puppy in an unused and sealed container and leave it at your window for three hours of the clock, quietly saying "Just as this puppy is kept alert and sleepless for my needs and use, so may you be subjected likewise, O

155

unyielding one. And just as this puppy is consumed by flame, so too may you be consumed, you Dog and Mounter. And may you seek me though I dismiss you and may you lap my liquids, white and red, though I repulse you, and may you smell my orifices and my depths though I chase you with stones so you collapse to the ground and pour forth your spittle and seed before me yet still I spurn you, and may I tread you underfoot though you beseech and howl a full seven days and nights, O menstrual and rutted, you whom I call though you do not come, whom I await at night while you slumber. Now thus. Now fus. Now mer and mors and mare. Lap yourself, bare yourself, animate yourself.

Thereupon, (after seven days have passed) you will sense his scent and presence and will have him before you, tied to a leash, ill-risen, unwashed and wan. And should you perceive his body trembling, then let it tremble. And should you hear his heart pounding, then let it pound. And should his gender's members and pudenda shudder, then let them shudder. And keep him standing there nine whole days, that he be sleepless on your account and be greatly assailed to your greater glory. On the ninth day, release him and have him render to you all the pleasures thrice in accordance with your will and wishes. Or feed him – that he may not die on you – and again put him on the leash and leave him to watch over you in the night, sleepless and blighted, as befits him.

If your love is of a feminine nature, heartless, merciless and aloof, and, an ardent paramour or faithful spouse, is in some other's charge, or parades unyoked and taunting so that you grieve at her very name and remain sleepless and unnourished while all along she plies you with empty vows and deceits, do not at all despair. If it be the sixth month, wait for the seventh day of the seventh month, the seventh hour of night prior to cockcrow. If it be the third month, wait for the fourth, the fourth day and so on and so forth. Thereupon, take a sacerdotal slate, blessed, or, for want of this, rabbit paper or vulture skin and spit upon this thrice, saying "I thus spit thrice, my Handmaid and Bitch, thrice upon thrice and thrice more that

I may come to possess you. I will drip droplets, you will shed streams, I spittle, you froth and grease to boot, above, below, before, behind you. Limada, Opouka, Eloe! O female creature, and ripe for purchase, may they sell you that I buy you, may they clothe you that I bare you, may they guard you that I rule you, Cunnu and Canne and Cadavra."

Having recited these sacred and awesome words and shuddering within, enter your bath in all your nakedness and carry out your ablutions crosswise and most decorously and, thereupon, remain as in the tomb, motionless, speechless and devoid of drink for three whole days, for you have suffered and would be gladdened, for you have loved and would be resurrected. And on the third day, rise up and again enter your bath and wash away your languish and take syrup of fragrant minirma juice and fatted calcha chaloui flour and savour it and smear it profusely upon your verge. And again take up the slate or paper and spit out your semen most profusely, saying "O behold how I discharge upon the breeze, my graceful girl and pride. Hail to you and behold how on your account I look to my three most secret stars. The one hungers, the other thirsts and the third would sleep. I set the first to sup, the second to imbibe, yet the third I set not to slumber upon its couch. For you shall come to find me now and forever. And may you be most feminine my fettered one that though I beat you with iron rods, you will hearken to no other save me, your only One. May you forget your abode for mine and renounce your bed for mine. And may all your body's limbs be mine, my property, my possessions. The outer, the inner, the black, the red, the concealed and apparent, the wet and the parched, every single one of them. I command you, I order you. Rise, Crawl. Stoop. Opened. Undone. Frenzied. Hungered. Famished. Now and Forever. Emerge vile blood and smell and bind. For I am your Present, your Past and your Future. Amen!"

Thereat, you will see a light, flickering and awesome, before which you will close your eyes slightly that you may not be blinded. And when a suitable time has elapsed and the light steadies, you will feel a woman's body, fully naked, entwined around you like a Bitch out of Hell as she humbly smells and laps you. Whereupon, take your seven hands, with their seven seals and your seven fettered feet and your seven unchristened verges and close with her. And sensually grasp your lady's breasts and pay homage to your love's nipples yet also to their rosy garland and partake of the milk within her and drain it. And drag out her sleep and nestle it within you. And grasp her heart and shake it that it may fall like a dry leaf on your account. And parched as you are, irrigate yourself with her liquids, and famished as you are in love's lair, plunder her beauty, and ugly and repulsive as you are, beautify yourself through her and shine radiant. And once you have satisfied all your needs, and your senses have supped and been appeased, grasp her waist and flanks and thighs (which the spouse has as his pride and the lover as his joy) and possess these in their length, breadth and depth. And ruthlessly open her pudendum, yet also her pudendum's pudendum, the upper and the lower, the down-looking, the unseen, the suspended, the fleshly and the notional, and stoke this same upright, full face, in stentorian tones. And when you grow weary and your amorous struggles abate, take a rope and bind her naked, and place her on the floor before your bed that she may guard you till you wake the next morn and may serve you again, as befits her.

29.
Concerning Erotic
Bedtime Stories

If the lady of your heart and dreams has been mollycoddled and, as one overly pampered, has from her homelife acquired infantile habits and ever seeks the caresses of her mother and sire and the cosseting of her brothers and neither wearies nor slumbers but keeps you awake till late and pesters you the night long, then before retiring to bed with her, do as nursemaids do with their infant charges and you will find thereby a little sleep and rest.

Take up your infant in your arms and bring her with laughter and play to your chamber and place her decorously and fully-clothed as she is upon your cot and between the cot's sheets purportedly to lie with her the night long. Thereupon (as you are arranging her), begin reciting to her an old tale told to you by your aged grandmother, supposedly that "Once upon a time there was a beautiful princess who was sick with sleep. She slept all night and all day and her father was unable to awaken her for sleep's steed had passed through the garden of her slumber in a fury and had eaten the flowers and greenery that awakens one each morning, and from that time she had remained in slumber and darkness. And many physicians and apothecaries came but were unable to awaken her, though she had her eyes wide open yet did not wake. And, anon, there arrived a Prince, though now poor from the loss of his realm, and he gazed upon the sleeping princess and rejoiced in her beauty so that his heart overflowed and he declared, Either I shall die, almighty God, or she will emerge from her slumber." At which point (as your lady reposes and listens to you), take her arms in feigned innocence and coaxingly and remove her upper camisole, then lift her legs and remove her lower garment, placing these on the edge of the cot to keep you warm.

This having been done, return to your tale and "Whereupon the Prince took up his staff and said to it, lead the way ahead and I shall follow behind you, that we may find sleep's steed and recover from it the greenery and flowers of her slumber for only thus will my sleeping beauty awake. And the young lad set off on his way, travelling three days forward and one back and on the fourth day he came to a gate fashioned all of gold."

At this juncture, bring your account to a halt and keep the prince waiting awhile before the gate of your narration and again artfully clasp her arms and legs and remove her bodice from beneath her arms and her bosom's gossamer lace together with the linen from her flanks and likewise place these beside you that they may perfume and incense you.

Then, as you are studiously kneeling upon the cot, take your infant in your arms and cradle her, as the waves cradle the sea and lull it, and turn your olfaction to your maiden's vulva, saying "O the Comb of your musk, O the canal of your liquids, O the current of the rivers' confluence that calls to me to enter and drown my grief. And so saying, discard your clothing, outer and inner, and bring your tongue to the well-springs of her breast and take three gulps of her milk that it may become one with your tongue.

Thereupon, return to the lad in your tale and "He then raised his staff to the golden gate and thrice pounded upon it shouting, O steed of sleep, cruel horse of slumber, come out for I have words to say to you. Yet he received no answer. And again he raised his staff and pounded upon the dark door and the doors and windows shook and the walls' foundations creaked. So great was the force of his pounding.

Three full days he knocked and thundered at the doors and on the third, there came from within a voice, neither of bird, nor horse, nor man, and it said, Who knocks and thunders so, and what does he want? Thereat, the lad let out a great cry, saying 'Tis I, the King of Glory. Raise the Gate! And the greenery that you took, give it back and the flowers beside, since my lady's garden is destitute and my sleeping Princess wakes not. And her father is unable to awaken her though her eyes be open. And again from within the voice answered, saying, And who pray is this King of Glory who knocks and thunders all night long and where is your authority, impoverished as you are? 'Tis I, he answered once more. And my authority is the fairness of my sleeping Princess, hence raise the gate. And he pounded with his staff most powerfully and the hills and springs all opened and castles crumbled in view, yet the steed stayed within, enraged."

Whereat, cradle her prudently once more and lull her and, while thus engaged, insert your tongue into her orifice that you may test her liquids, lest her waters flow in the hours of sleep and she become wet on you. Then, artfully shake her well-springs and call to her water that this may flow from her hills and valleys and descend to her orifice and that, overflowing, she may say to you, O my Master, now my water has arrived at my orifice and I am in need. And you will fetch her silver pot and take your heart's desire and set her upon the pot as did her mother, saying to her, O release your water, my fragrance, lest sleep befall you and you become wet on me in the night.

At that same moment, as the hissing of her water echoes in the silver pot, so too the steed's snorting will be heard, for it has sensed her odour and emerged. Whereupon, take up your tale anew while she is sitting wholly bared, though be mindful lest she fall asleep and tumble to the ground, and "Thus the lad replied and again pounded with his staff and the gates opened and through the foliage the steed appeared snorting at the odour of the sleeping girl. The steed laughed haughtily at the lad and said, If you desire that I give back the greenery and flowers of her slumber, what is there of gain for me? And the unsleeping lad answered, Take what you will. At this the steed retorted, I will take from you your sleep for the rest of your life. And the lad said, Take it.

Thereafter, the steed grew calm and the lad mounted it and plucked abundant greens and whites and reds and much foliage for her slumber. And upon his arrival at the palace, he said, keep back all of you! For I have brought the greens and yellows and whites and blues and foliage to fill the garden of my heart's desire that she may smell them and awaken as a living being once more. Though I shall be assailed without rest in my desolation. And forthwith he took up his sleeping princess, O my precious, my sleeping beauty, and he brought her to the blooming garden and she straightway emerged from her slumber and found her light and glory and asked for food and drink.

At this point, for by now your lady will have discharged her water, take up your cosseted lady and bring her in your arms to the bath and bathe her wholly and lather her and perfume her till her tiny head droops from the perfume's scent. Then take your now drowsy infant and bring her again to your chamber and your cot and tell to her this last tale of noble sleep in which this same supposedly comes with his sheets and takes all the sweet-smelling and well-scrubbed babies and brings them to verdant lands and flourishing gardens and, when they have grown up, returns them again to their mothers and sires. Thereupon, when she has shut her eyes, it is time for you too, if you so wish, to lie at her side for a little respite. And should you wish to sleep, then do so. And should you wish to lie awake, then do so. Yet be mindful lest your infant wake deep into the night and begin to cry. Wherefore, gently cradle her from time to time and lull her till daytime comes once more and you again rise to attend to the gentle and graceful cause of your sleeplessness.

30.
Concerning Places of Travail yet likewise of Coition

Firstly, know that just as the earth produces its fruits exceeding well when worked by some local, for he grasps and masters its nature, so too if your coition is in a familiar and intimate place, you will be more happily rewarded and your pleasure will be profuse. Therefore, if you toil night and day in a certain place of work and are seized by an overwhelming desire for coition, yet are at a loss to find some other place appropriate for immediate copulation and delight, proceed as follows that you may know undiminished pleasure yet not lose the profit from your toil. Since areas of toil are sundry, so sundry too are the forms of coition in each workplace. Thus we shall refer to but three places of work which are most conducive to coition; to wit, the perfumery, the bakery and the quiet reading-room, and let workers and amorists everywhere take heed and act accordingly.

If you earn your livelihood as a busy perfumer and a most amorous lady (whether known to you or unknown is of no matter) enters your shop, wishing to purchase scents and sensuous perfumes and, upon her entering, you feel within her liquids gleaming playfully and the eyes of your verge open wide and your saliva flowing, above and below, leave your counter and cash register at once and go up to her, wrapped as you are in your apron and say to her "O melodious and delectable creature! You have entered my perfumery yet scent I have none to extract for you my gentle lady. Regard how for so long I have been preparing oil of divine and godly myrrh from aromatic resin, from Greek cedar, musk rose, broad-leaved jasmine, marjoram and wild mint. And though I work ceaselessly and have innumerable phials of this perfume, the oil remains unwholesome for it lacks one essential ingredient and I am at a loss. Come then with me behind this curtain and aid me, for I recognise in your odour the ingredient for my needs and my eyes have seen my salvation and opened wide."

So saying, most humbly take your odoriferous lady and drive away all your customers (as supposedly you have to tend to your production) and enter into the workshop of your perfumery. Therein, kindle a blazing fire and set upon it a copper distillation kettle and cast inside it all the afore-mentioned aromatics. Position the distillation pipe so that it passes through cooling water and allow its end to open into a small shallow bowl. Then (while waiting for it to boil) spread upon your couch bluebells and bunches of wild sea-violets (viola alba marina) together with white hyacinths – elsewhere known as Kretan sea-blooms – and disrobe your maiden to her inner depths and set her upon these, as bare as when her mother bore her. Then bending over her, clothed as you are and wearing your apron, deeply inhale her odour above and below, front and rear, that you may investigate her every fount of fragrance. And at the place that most pleases you, remain for a goodly time and take stock of it, yet also generously lubricate her fair skin and every hairy nook and gently yet unfailingly fondle all her passages and tiny orifices. Once you see her growing ani-mated as in dreaming (while the flame leaps and the ingredients bubble and boil) bare yourself entirely and stand over her as though incensing her from the vessel of your privates. Then moisten all her dry parts and diligently wipe the wet, and advance wherever she withdraws and persist wherever she resists till she is fully warmed and her fluids flow and her liquids and perspiration merge with the aromatics on the couch.

And as the vapours from the boiling kettle rise and con-dense inside the pipe's coolness, you will observe the distilled essence trickling drop by drop into the bowl. At that moment, either have your tongue in your lady's fragrant cavities, there-by catching her juices, or insinuate your verge into her swad-dling pudenda (*ala recto*, if such is your desire, *ala verso*) that you may collect her oils. Thus doing, gather the ingredient that you lack and let it trickle into the bowl together with the extract from the distillation.

If you are an able perfumer yet also a lusty and dextrous

amorist, your profit from each cohabitation and distillation will amount to two to three ounces of choice translucent oil. If you are less able, then be satisfied with just one ounce, yet take care not to adulterate the extract on account of quantity lest the preparation lose its potency and cloud. Wherefore, while with your lady you drain each other, take care to have beside you sufficient glass phials – of green or violet colour – and fill these, using cotton to catch the mixture. Then present your assistant with as much oil as she desires and name the rest after her and sell it most expensively.

To the bakery come many ladies daily, so that if in truth you are an able baker and dextrous kneader, you will find pleasure in sundry ways. Hence, bide your time and when a fair and enticing lady enters your store and torments you with her mien and blights you with her obstinacy, approach her in supplication and entreaty, saying to her "O my celestial vessel! O my heavenly water! Regard how these long years I have been a baker, yet today my dough will not rise and my neighbours will revile my humble cakes. I beseech you, therefore, my blessed bounty, come into my kneeding room for my dough is sallow and my trough is cold, assist me with your flame and your breath."

So saying, ply your prime-kneader with blandishments and lead her to the room where lies the mixture, whether of wheat or barley. Then (having shut the door behind you) take her hands and rinse them in rosewater and barley-sugar solution that they may be sweet and fragrant. Remove her shoes and likewise wash her feet most humbly and dry them well with a soft Venetian towel. Then spread out a handsome purple rug, thick lest your dough and damsel grow cold, and set the trough upon a couch or bed so that as she kneads, she will bend most low for you and her fair body will charm with its swaying. As she thrusts her hands into the dough and her fingers grow sticky, swiftly come upon her from behind, saying "O my fair mistress, I fear lest you stain your dress." So saying, grasp the hem of her dress and likewise of her petticoat and lift these, pinning them high to her waist. Then artfully grasp her linen and remove it completely that her haunches may be revealed, lighting the house.

While ever she toils in front, you too will ply and grapple from the rear and either you will thoroughly inhale her hidden depths or you will insinuate your tongue into her fat and pliant parts, ever poking your verge into the dough to test the thickness of the mix. Once you see the two mixtures becoming similar in consistency, fragrance and taste, take up your trough and set it upon the floor for safety's sake. Whereupon, remove every piece of clothing from your assistant and take two tiny cushions that she may kneel yet not grow weary. And, as the able baker that you are, teach her how to lean fully over the dough and immerse her arms most deeply. And when, anon, the mixture hardens sufficiently and the paste turns thickly in her hands, kneel undone as you are behind her and, having lodged your verge in her vulva's canal, afix yourself to her and knead in unison.

Set all the cakes that you kneaded with her prior to discharge, viz. while still unemptied of your seed, upon a tray and bake them in haste for these same rise rapidly with heat. As for the remainder that you kneaded with your seed released, there is no urgency. And while the cakes are baking and emitting their sweet smell, scour your trough to remove the remainder of the dough and place your kneader within and, taking warm spring water, bathe her fair body entirely in all her length and depth. Then take aromatic oils (rose oil and oils of valerian and jasmine) and anoint her that she may shine and glow and again clothe her decorously and kiss her hands and feet for you were cold and unrisen yet these raised and warmed you. And when you take out the cakes and your neighbours delight in their smell and appearance, take seven of these and cross them reverently, breaking them into four parts, and distribute them to the poor and hungry. And give praise to the Lord of Bread and the Lady of the Bread Shop that they deemed you worthy to fill and be filled.

All the cakes thus baked will emerge resplendent and most delectable. Sometimes, however, as has been observed in kneading of this kind, the cakes kneaded after the first discharge of seed are somewhat humbler than the rest, though in quality no way inferior.

IF you are a studious reader yet also seasoned amorist and you spend much time in reading-rooms, neglect not the benefit of knowledge nor yet the delights of Aphrodite's arts. Wherefore, avoid whatever is pedantic and insipid (for this has ruined many a scholar and tutor) and, as you have your eyes open in the books, so also keep open the eyes of your verge and your other organs. When from afar you espy and strongly smell a lady entirely engrossed in her study, yet you are impassioned by her fair figure and beset by her fragrance, straightway leave your seat and move beside her, for supposedly the lighting is poor and your vision is impaired.

When sufficient time has elapsed and your bodies become reconciled in their proximity, lift up your tome and softly and humbly ask her "My studious lady, here I cannot grasp the meaning of this passage. Grant me the light of your learning and wisdom for tomorrow my Tutor will question me and revile me for my ignorance. I read in these lines, "*O feet, o legs, o thighs for which I justly died, o buttocks, o bosom*, and I understand all these, yet that *O comb* I fail to comprehend its meaning. Does it mean, I wonder, the comb in her hair. Yet I deem it unbecoming for the poet to enumerate a trinket together with her physical charms. Or is it that this too is a true part of her body?" And, so saying, move yet closer to her and boldly clasp her foot and say "Regard the foot". And similarly clasp the flesh of her legs and thighs that inflame you, and her flanks and breasts to their very milk, and say to her "Regard these your limbs, yet your comb I see not, and who will show me, ignoramus that I am, if not you who are most fair and wise!"

Ply her then with blandishments and lead her to a secluded and quiet reading room and bare her to the roots of her hair. Thereupon, remove all your own garments and place these either upon the desk together with the open lexicons and reference books or beside the desk that they may serve as a place of learning and study. Thus, when you study her *ala recto*, viz. wide-open and from the fore, and you riffle through her

171

beside the Mega-Lexicon of the Greek Language, be sure not only to grasp her points but also to learn by heart her passages, and digest everything learnedly and comprehensively through your senses and likewise through your sensibility.

And when you journey down from the upper to the lower and come to the place commonly known as the Mound of Venus (or in dialect as the Mont) and you stoop and fully savour the parched and wooded areas, bring your tongue and dip into the Greek fonts, in the hollows and fragrances that in older times were known collectively as the Wide Straits. And as you drain and comb the reefs, you will feel, being as you are a linguist and lover of Greece, the teeth of her comb opening melodiously like the comb of a loom or lyre, or like the bivalve marine mollusc. And since you are by nature conscientious and studious, bring your member to her comb, saying "O my Coiffeuse and Instructress! Regard how I am unkempt and dishevelled and the time for the lesson is nigh and how shall I enter thus untidy into my Tutor's class? Pray do not refuse to groom me and comb me diligently and carefully to my roots. And take up your member, aroused and agitated as it is, and prudently insert it between the teeth of her comb and do not end your lesson in the art of beautification save only after the passing of two hours of undisturbed instruction and three intervals.

Should you study her *ala verso*, viz. from the back, the rear and the rump, do not neglect to examine all her passages, the difficult and the meaningful, for the beginning of all wisdom is in the examination of terms. And when you have pored over every margin and lacuna with touch, taste and smell, have her assume the posture of the Sphinx and proceed as above. And when you are thoroughly combed and spruced, take your fair instructress and dress her diligently and comb her fine hair and present her with all your lexicons and volumes, now useless, yet give praise to her, for you were unlearned and learned, ungroomed and were groomed. Then again shut yourself up in your study and investigate your life alone, till deep into the night.

31.
On How to Render
Your Lady most Desirable
to Strangers

Though it be the prime concern of amorists to take pleasure in their lady and thus to find contentment, men more gracious and gallant, who are driven by unbridled passion and concupiscence, should not only enjoy their paramour or spouse, but yet assist and render her that she may appear exceedingly desirable and delightful to others besides. Thus, upon consulting ancient scripts, we learn of such gracious and gallant men who so worshipped their ladies that, unable to endure the passion and pleasure, either wandered through the streets, cafés and concert halls, extolling their lady's beauty, or who invited into their homes total strangers, unfortunate in love and uncomely in form, revealing to them the manifest yet also hidden charms of their heart's desire. Wherefore, if you wish to be reckoned a most gallant man and a prudent and noble-minded lover, see to it that by your own hand you render your lady radiant that she may sparkle most alluringly in the eyes and hearts of others and thus be glorified. For we light not the candle to put it under a bushel, but to reveal it. Should, however, you lack the gallant persuasion of exquisite desire and belong to the lower order of lovers, sit and guard her beauty in your foolishness and fear till she herself reveals her hidden and private charms and in a way both unbecoming and imprudent. Equally, if you are miserly and give not your gift consummately, it were better that you remain where you are in the lowly and humble order.

Arise then early at a time in early Summer (natural or notional), when the days are yet becoming longer and the air's purity is invigorating, and rouse from her slumbers the paramour that inflames you or your spouse and say to her "O my beauteous and my eyes' torment! I dreamed a dream and saw that together we must come atop a pleasant hill which many frequent. For these same ones are desolate and thirst for love and though they have eyes, yet they have nothing to look upon. Come, let me bring you to this mount, for this figment of my wits has appointed you, my Precious."

When her sleepiness has passed and your lady has shaken off its fetters and her limbs shine now fair amid the sheets, take her up like to an infant and bathe and wash her thoroughly in heated water, cleansing her body's rivulets from the remnants of her reveries and erasing the night's traces. Next, have ready ordered precious and expensive garments to match her body's hues, viz. trusseaux of fine gossamer from Venetian lands, silks from Cathay, smooth velvet from the Orient and precious and regal gowns from the populated towns of the Occident. And clothe her body with due propriety in keeping with the splendour of her stature and as befits her arms and legs and pudenda, that what is apparent may be concealed and what is buried may be vaunted. And hang upon her bangles and earrings of gold and pearl, of sapphire and amethyst most conducive to pleasure. Then take perfumes pleasing to her senses and her smell, yet apply these with some measure, that her body may smell fragrant with the essences and the essences may merge with her liquids and the perspiration from her arms, and her inner, newly-worn linen may be permeated with both.

When, anon, she has become most inwardly beautiful and perfect in imagination and word, escort her, adorned and desirable as she is, and climb the mount. Once there, cry out in a gladly and stentorian voice (though slightly plaintive) and call to the forsaken and destitute from the far ends of the earth and instruct them to sit humbly upon the ground. And when many have thus gathered and a sufficient multitude of men, women and children has arrived, wait for the sun to blaze and for the heavens to spout fiery tongues and for her fair body to be ringed with splendour and radiance. Thereupon (allow some time to elapse) ply your heart's desire with blandishments and bid her stand upright in the shape of a cross, for the hour of her glorification has come. And taking hold of her outer garment, in which you clad her, gently remove it and set it before the multitude. Thereafter (when the flapping of her breast abates), take hold of her inner garment and remove it and set this similarly before the multitude. Then (a suitable time having passed) take hold of her bodice in which her mother had clothed her to protect her breasts and her breasts' nipples throughout her whole life long, yet also the odour of her armpits and the gentle roots of her perspiration. Take hold of this bodice and pull it gently from her and lay her open for her breasts to emerge into the glimmering light and flap them in the breeze in the fashion of a dove.

Thereat, an "Ahh" will ring out from the lips of the simple folk and you will call them blessed for, poor and thirsty as they were, they will eat and drink that which was their desire. And when their "Ahh" subsides, grasp her petticoat with your fingertips and pull it from her and shake it in the breeze that the crumbs of her flesh may fall to the hungry. Then take her inner linen with which her mother and sire covered her modesty and bare her before all present and reveal her thighs and the flesh of her thighs and her flanks and the air of her flanks and her pudenda, worshipped by you in both mind and spirit. And again say to her "O my Malady and Scourge, open wide your arms, my lady, that the air may grow stronger. Stoop, my willow, that the planet might move. Bend, my fairest, a little to the fore, bend now a little to the rear that the multitude may take pleasure in the ways of your mounds. Open all your rivulets and reveal the mysteries of your upper and lower lips and the well-springs of your liquids in accordance with their smells and savours."

Thereat, you will again hear an "Ahh" from the humble folk and you will grasp the lofty sun and turn its rays upon her legs and upon the chink between her legs and say to her air "O immaculate air, that flows from the vulva of my lady on account of my scorched limbs, blow over these humble and ignorant folk and make them rejoice, for they have loved yet have not love, and have known desire yet attained it not."

Straightway, you will see the fabric of the heavens shaking and the wind will rise from her body's peaks and vales and ridges and ravines, and her roseries will bloom together with all her orchards and arbours, and her gardens and evergreens and fruit-trees and the down of her eyebrows and the nodes of

177

her branches and her body will sprout leaves and bear fruit and a roar will be heard from the multitude and they will glorify her for she was glorified by you and will desire her most greatly, for you also did desire her on their behalf.

When all this has come to pass and you have divided her clothes among the multitude, lend her the air of your wits which is called civil and civilised and inner wealth of convictions and inspire her, for she will journey naked and in her fleshliness to barbarous lands. Open up the coffers of your lofty meditations, which for years upon years you have amassed, and give these unsparingly and lavishly, for it was on her account that you acquired wisdom and it is to her that these same are due. And place in her hands a Greek lute or outi or kithera, and, taking her fingers, teach her the lays of your forefathers for these will safeguard her in foreign lands and allow her to disappear into the multitude of humble folk and into the hands of their hands and into the eyes of their eyes. And, thereupon, all will desire and call her blessed. And you will return home alone and keep vigil for three long days.

32.
On Ways by which Love Lost May Be Lamented

Although the most noble loves end well, viz. at their allotted hour (otherwise the passion is protracted and sours), lamenting for love lost is neither unnatural nor futile and oft times people unable to support the separation have lost their wits; nevertheless, it is neither befitting nor proper for love's image to dull through excessive lamentation or for love's relish to lose its savour. Know, then, that just as carnal cohabitation is a noble form of art, yet most difficult, so also ending love's grief requires strength of soul and great humility. Know also that though there exist sundry ways to grieve for vain and illusory love, the most expedient, as adjudged by those versed in such matters, are but few. Thus, in a treatise recorded in the mystical tongue of the Sabacthani, viz. of the forsaken, we read the following: since the main places of recollection (*zikran*) in this false and futile world are three, viz. the earth, the sea and the winds of the air, so also in these places are to be found the main scales (*maquem*) which raise one to the level of perfect lamentation in the way and the word of the gnostic vedá (*taqasim i'layali*). Here, then, is where one so forsaken should turn, and in each place of recollection in keeping with the kind and nature of his love, let him weep and lament. Yet this he must do this secretly and in all modesty and not in common view and ostentatiously.

Myself wishing to offer solace to the separated, I have collected the more substantial and expedient of the plethora of mystic readings and, to the best of my abilities, have set down in our native tongue the three highest scales of lamentation and consolation, so that should one in truth have need, he may study them and ascend them to his greater benefit.

I. First scale, of the earth

IF the love that eludes and assails you acquired substance amid the elements of your earth and you found your lady (paramour or spouse) sprouting in your soily elements and branching in sundry directions, just as ivy around weaker trees, do not imprudently allow your tears to flow to her roots for ease of watering and lamentation. Nor take up an axe to cruelly destroy her rustlings. Do not act thus imprudently and deceive yourself that ostensibly you encounter temporary respite from your dolour. Know that a woman who has sprouted within you and flourished in your soil and moisture, yet now gives her flowers and fruit elsewhere, will never be satisfied no matter how much you irrigate her with your fluids, both lacteal and sanguineous, for you are her secret spring and hidden well. Instead, prepare yourself as does the good husbandman, who having nurtured an exquisite tree in the narrowest of plots and seeing it straining to surpass its confines and shed its fruit in other fields, resolves of necessity to carefully uproot it and plant it elsewhere that it may rejoice in the utmost and shine radiantly.

Whereupon, prepare whatever necessary and come to that most narrow garden known as the *maqam* of Gethsemane, viz. the place and scale of perpetual lamentation and mourning. Arrive at the garden in the darkness of night, at some moon-less hour, and have yourself fittingly bedecked and bejewelled in honour of your love. Enter into the farthest reaches of the garden and all around inscribe a black lead circle which you may not cross and break out. Sit and keep vigil for five hours of the clock (from the ninth hour of night to the second morning hour) and lend your whole spirit to the blossoming of your love and ascend repeatedly and prudently from its roots to its leaves, and then again descend till you see it suspended and radiant. Fondle regularly though delicately the evergreen pudenda (which blighted you that they might blossom) and trace the folds of your foliaceous lady and riffle through them just as of old you would close with her in all her nakedness. At the third morning hour, just before the cock crows and you forget yourself, take out with due propriety all your ruins, tangible and notional, and take your phials of tears carefully that not one drop be lost and set these all upon the ground. And should you discover anything murky and dull, clean and attend to it appropriately, for soon her recollection will come and it is unbecoming that she should find you unsightly when she descends from out the clouds.

When you espy your sapling arriving from the heavens and offering you the cup of your tears, saying "O my lord, my husbandman and garden. Take this cup and, with your tears, fill it to the brim and pour it upon my tiny roots, for I have longed for you, my unjustly scorned beloved." Accept the cup with due respect though do not fill it yet for the time is inopportune. But take up your spade and hoe and betake yourself in imagination to the place where your lady lives and amorously delights in the breath of her harvesters and there dig a pit three feet in depth and four wide. And fashion the pit so that it be narrow above and wider below that the roots may spread out quickly, and gather up the dry leaves and straws that rustle within you and burn them in the pit that these may provide benefit and warmth during the transplanting. Only then should you return to the place of your heart where your rooted and false love rustles, and dig most deeply and take care to extract all the roots and rhizoids and shoots and do this in haste lest a chill comes to blight them. And having uprooted your tree, take bile from your bile and blood from your blood and smear the roots on account of worms and pests injurious to trees and bring it and plant it in the other pit.

When you have stoutly planted it and embedded it with soft and fertile soil, stick reeds and oleanders and thistles all around its roots lest the sapling be eaten by animals and fail to flourish. And then, as the sun shines upon your completed work, take the vessels of your tears and shatter them all upon its roots and clasp the cup given you by the seductress and fill it from your eyes and give it to the tree to drink. Thereafter, gather up your tools and return the way you came yet turn not to gaze upon the place of forsaking, but bid farewell to the sun and birds of the air and depart.

On the third day (but only in bright weather), come to your freshly-planted tree and again water it most generously from the well-springs of your body. Yet neglect not to speak to it, for trees sense the voices of their husbandmen, and recount to it the tale of the One who had within him a leafy and fruitful tree, but hard times came and the tree was in danger of withering and it spread far its roots and surrendered its leafage to the wind. And how this same man carefully uprooted it and carried it to a more auspicious place and planted it. And how, though it now flourishes and rustles in another's field, he passes beneath it and addresses it and takes much pride in it and he has with him a watering can and waters it.

ALTERNATIVELY: If your love was as an oak in the hills and the wild Thracian wind blew and rendered it twigs and branches, do as the lamenters of deciduous trees. When these same, in truth delectable and erotic creatures yet extremely proud and haughty, feel the infirmity of their foliage, they scale lonely trees where, all year long, they sit without sustenance or beverage, yet they neither weep nor lament improprietously, but sit and wait till they become like to the leaves and branches of the tree and till winter and a strong northerly comes and breaks the branches, so committing them to the abyss and the void.

II. Second scale, of the sea

IF the love that besets you arose in the sea foam but a strong northerly blew and swept it off and a choppy southerly sank it, take care not to dive imprudently that thus you might unfetter it from the depths of your heart and it might rise into the daylight as it was before. Nor sit upon a rock and embitter the waves with the streams of your eyes, for loves born and sunk in the waves are thus nourished with bitter brine and drownings. Hence it is most dangerous for one to lament at the sea's edge for the level of the waters may well rise and he be drowned. Instead of this, if in truth you wish to drag her from your depths to give her freedom and release, then proceed as follows. Choose a moonless and unlit night and betake yourself to a place beside the sea known in the Grecian tongue as the "Sea Sore", viz. the Scale of drowning and sinking. Have with you a wooden effigy of your drowned lady and carry in a cage the mountain bird known as the corbie, which has as its natural song the lament. And see to it that you are most elegantly dressed and bedecked, as those in mourning dress and bedeck themselves.

When seven hours of the night have elapsed and you see the wooden image softening in your hands, you will feel the creature trembling and fluttering. Thereupon, remove your fine shirt and dress the effigy carefully that it may not grow cold, and take all your finery and give this to your illusion and idol, thus remaining impoverished and naked in the way of ascetics and anchorites. Then sing within yourself mystically, yet resoundingly, the musical scale known as *mizhar*, viz. He who reveals the cause of the apparent, and thus sit and chant for four long hours. Then, either stirred by your heart's ebullition or gripped by an old recollection, the effigy will of its own accord begin to float and will sail off into the midst of the sea, as though They call to me and I must go, my Dove, and come let us go together. Yet do nothing but wave the kerchief from your breast in the breeze, saying Hail and Farewell, my wanderer, as those embittered by the world do, and bid your distant love god speed.

Once the image is far gone and has vanished in the distance, assume the position of valediction and remain in your place for three whole days, with neither sustenance nor sleep, till your reason and heart clears from the profit of the world and you are left as a lone stalk in a harvested field. Thereat, all the sea's haze will dissolve and your every bound thought will head out to sea. And the water will boil and the heavens will flash and you will see thunderbolts falling all around you that will shake the earth and startle the sea. Release, then, the corbie from its cage and set it to fly as if in a sea garden and entreat it to sing for you with great sweetness, since your spirit has grown heavy from all the lamentation. And when you feel lightened from your burdens, cast yourself into the black waters and swim three miles and three more and thrice times three, stark naked as you are, yet have with you a flaxen sack three measures long and one in width.

When you find yourself amid the black water, in the position of the Diver, halt and place your body in the sack and sew your own self into the sack and allow yourself to sink thus bound. Thereupon, you will begin to descend into a sea, white and smooth like glass, and though you will indeed be below the sea, you will soar beneath the heaven's vault and you will now feel whatever of yours has drowned and sunk in former times as winged hosts all around you, as undiminished and unquestionable flames.

Thus you shall sink for in excess of one thousand fathoms, shut within your sack yet with your eyes wide open to the view. It is then that suddenly you will espy, rising from your heart's deep depths, the vain and illusory image of your love, the same which you bedecked and animated and to which you granted freedom and release. And as the image comes towards you breathing radiantly and coquettishly, you will see the new moon rising and the beams of the lifeless moon will be shed on her form and she will acquire movement and the sense of a real body, like to the fair body that of old you held in your arms, but the mistral blew and dissolved it and the levanter arose and swept it away.

Remain there suspended amidst the black lake encircling you and allow the rising image to pass beside you, now radiant like to a distant fantasy. And when she passes proudly and ascends sufficiently, allow yourself to sink anew, though ever casting your gaze upwards and taking pride. And you will see that the black water will overflow with her radiance and your moonclad lady will rise like a column of light into the air, reaching towards the stars. Thereupon, allow yourself to plummet straight down and when your feet touch bottom, open up the sack in which you are sewn and emerge with joy upon the shore and sandy beach. And as you touch land, put it into your mind that ostensibly you are sitting at night time in a place known as the "Sea Sore" and you will straightway be holding in your hands the wooden effigy of one you had and lost, and have with you shut in a cage a bird known in dialect as the Corbie which has as its sole song the lament.

Sit in this spot for three long days, without sustenance or sleep, and then, when you feel relieved of your burden and the profits of this illusory and vain world, cast yourself into the waters and have with you a flaxen sack and sew yourself inside with due caution and return again to where you began.

ALTERNATIVELY: Whosoever has lost the love (male or female) that he once chanced to dream of and, on awakening, no longer possesses, and he weeps inconsolably for this same, let him reflect that for dreamt loves, there exists no remedy for the pain. As is remarked by those well-versed, dreams are like to paper most fine and white, which cannot be divided according to thickness nor be rendered into two identical sheets because of its fineness and fragility. It may, of course, be cut up into strips and rent in two, but this is of no benefit whatsoever. Wherefore, leave the paper intact and unwritten as it is, yet do not moisten it undecorously with your tears, nor weep for it often, but in time of utmost need, bring it into the sun and set yourself to deciphering the unwritten till you are versed in reading this.

III. Third scale, of the air

SINCE the aerial place is full of the spirits of the holy angels and the shades of songsters, known in the Grecian tongue as Seirenes, so also love that sprouted in this diaphanous and intangible place is mixed with angelic and musical essence. It is in its nature, therefore, not only to deceive and delude you, but also to be eternally drawn by the incorporeal and spirited. As such, it tends ever to depart towards the infinity of the ether, fashioning music and producing sounds, and to this end it removes your air and life's breath and respiration. Wherefore, if such a love, illusory and musical, has befallen you, allow it to flutter and screech without hindrance (without weeping or entreaties on your part) and have care for this one thing only, how with your air and breath it may sing and breathe. So be wary, and instead of lamenting and breaking your fetters that supposedly in this way you will tread your path now liberated, do rather as befits the abandoned and forsaken, who though leaving behind their bad blood and travelling far and distant, are yet close to it and savour it deep within.

When, therefore, you realise that in vain your spirit is wasting and your body's particles are decomposing in the heaven's vault, yet without due rhythm and order, know that the discordance and disharmony of your love is governing you and is deranging you. Hence, the time has come to prepare and acknowledge the same. Wait then for some sweet summer hour, preferably morning time, when the bushes are all heard to sing and the streams to echo. Whereupon, open wide your door and show yourself, dressed regally in your crimsons and violets, perfumed and radiant, as befits one about to set out on a distant journey. Then close the door behind you once and for all and venture forth into the town square and come first to the place where in times past your love was conceived. There (view it as a threshing floor), incense the breeze and air your ballads as best you can, albeit artlessly and ingenuously, such as "Ah, you my eternal love and Bane," or "O my world of gossamered and ardent air." Then, open exceeding wide your eyes till your light darkens and, though you see, you will be blinded and lost.

Whereupon, leave behind all your possessions, acquired and coveted. And with them the verdant buds of the earth and every flower and the tender shoots' calyces. And the river waters and the spring waters (the babbling and frothy), renounce also the birds' courses and the beasts' lairs, the birth of goats and the nativity of the lambs. Leave all these and have this one thing alone with you: a looking glass to keep your image lest in your solitude you lose your human form. And take to the road for two score days and ten, without sustenance, beverage or shelter and wretched like a savage outcast.

And having journeyed a thousand miles thrice and thrice a

188

thousand more, come at last and take refuge in a mountainous and arid place known in the tongue of the goodly Roumis as Kitha-I-raon, viz. the musical scale of perpetual recollection. Remain there till one hundred and one hundred more and one hundred and sixty degrees of the House of the Zodiac have full passed and calm yourself. Then choose a white rock and carve out a column to a height of two and twenty yards, well-wrought, most difficult to scale, the tip of which is in the clouds and the base in the soil and earth. And set upon its top a wooden basket, like to a crow's-nest, and weave an aerial ladder and climb this same and assume the position of the stylites, viz. hanging from the heavens and banished by the earth. Then cast the ladder down and, in this fashion, allow a great length of time to pass, breathing normally. And, now and again, gaze into the looking glass lest you forget yourself. And remain like this till your extremities are perfectly deformed and your limbs are scattered to the winds in the way of celestial cicadas.

When, anon, you see reflected in your eyes your image as an infant and, hungry, you seek your mother's milk, know that your asceticism and desiccation is over. Yet do not descend from the basket imprudently nor take the path of your return crawling on all fours. Remain high in the element of air, and alone send your spirit down like to the mountain hawk that falls upon the hens leaving only feathers and down behind. And when, swaddled and wretched, you arrive at the gate of your house and someone asks "Who pray are you, swarthy stranger?" or "What might you want here?", reply in riddle and image that "I was here and have returned, for the blood and sounds of the womb have called to me." These are the limits of a man's knowledge and a son's complex, and from the portal will emerge a young bride and you will recognise her as the woman whom you loved of old and who abandoned you before the wind's three ways. This then is she. And straightway she will open her chamber to you, having loosed her lovely hair, and lutes and songs and hymeneals will resound in the streets and lanes. And as you enter overwhelmed, let out an infant's screech, so loud that from the cry your eyes fall out.

189

End this practised lament consummately well but no other. And upon finishing and finding yourself again perched within your crow's-nest, expiring and hymenopterous, you will see yourself now steadily evaporating into the air, like incense over an altar. And you will hear heavenly music from your bosom, "Eii, Eii, Aii, Aii," and your name being clearly called as you remember Who you were and Who you have become. Then, as you vanish bodiless into the vastness of the ether and your bones sprout and resound below in the woods and ravines, your deceptive and illusory love will come up beside you and say to you, "O my lord, give me your spirit that it may be my spirit and your breath that I may breathe." And this you will do unfalteringly, giving thanks to the hosts of angels and orders of songsters (for it was from you that they took breath and sang). And wipe away the misty tears from your eyes for true love should not be defiled by mourning, but be lauded by the innocent tongues of sparrows and by the lowly cicadas, the least of creatures, as for this they were born on earth, to ascend and depart the world, singing.

Thereupon, allow your spirit to depart in glory, desiccated and dry atop the column and its basket, content that you were worthy of such a love. And advance into the seventy-seven harmonies of your forefathers, surrendering yourself to the wind's grip, yet beholding to the sombre graces and songless muses. And as your music, perfected now as it is, becomes harmonised with the music of the divine utterances, humble yourself, as still a casuist and unversed, though something of a musician and hymnodist. From the fervour of your sound, you will be rendered bloodless, fleshless and hollow. And rise up, as one almost and virtually arrived, yet still far below the footstools of the holy angels and musical spirits, the sweet-sounding and seductive, known in Greek as Seirenes, viz. flimsy and futile.

And so ended the present treatise
In the early hours of the Sabbath
The work complete I found sleep
By a rocky precipice, Praise be.

THE AUTHOR

Yoryis Yatromanolakis was born in 1940 on the Greek island of Crete. He is the Professor of Ancient Greek at the University of Athens.

The publication of his third novel *The History of a Vendetta* in 1983 (Dedalus translation 1991) established him as one of Greece's most important 20th century novelists. It was awarded the First Greek National Prize for Literature and the Nikos Kazantzakis Prize for Literature. His fourth novel (Greek edition published in 1993) was translated into English by Dedalus as *A Report of a Murder* in 1995.

Dedalus will publish Yatromanolakis' first novel *Leimonario* in 2000.

THE TRANSLATOR

David Connolly has a first degree in Ancient, Medieval and Modern Greek and a Ph.D. in The Theory and Practice of Literary Translation. Since 1979 he has lived in Greece, working first at the British Council in Athens as Head of Translation and then at the Ionian University of Corfu as a lecturer in Literary Translation.

His translations include works by Vrettakos, Odysseus Elytis, Kiki Dimoula and Nikos Engonopoulos.

A Report of a Murder – Yoryis Yatromanolakis

The murder of his Professor by a postgraduate physics student during a lecture at Crete University in November 1990 shocked Greece. Many found Yatromanolakis' novel based on the event equally shocking, as he seemed to have more sympathy for the murderer than the victim and transposed his crime to the world of myth. *A Report of a Murder* has the same teasing style as *Tristram Shandy* as we enter the author's labyrinth and share in the novel's sense of tragic inevitability and eternal recurrence.

"Though steeped in the language of science and presented as a 'scientific' enquiry, and despite its detached, sometimes almost callous tone, *A Report of a Murder* is nevertheless a novel which is deeply romantic in spirit. It is the romance of the ancient legend, whose themes are of such grandeur that the lives of individuals can seem insignificant by comparison. The rhetorical tone (often laced with irony and humour) and freely shifting perspective between the scientific and the mystical are what lends the book its unique quality . . . Sombre, meticulous and unsettling, it is an epic for our time."

Andrew Crumey

£8.99 ISBN 1 873982 12 7 220p B.Format

The History of a Vendetta – Yoryis Yatromanolakis

The History of a Vendetta won the first Greek National Prize for Literature and the Nikos Kazantzakis Prize in 1983.

A murder in a small Cretan village: its motive and the fortunes of two families reflect the history of the Greek nation in the early part of the twentieth century. A magical, intricate tale, rich in peasant myth and narrated in the detached yet ultimately moving style of a modern Herodotus.

"*The History of a Vendetta* is a substantial artistic achievement. Yatromanolakis tells his tale with grace, patience and mastery, gradually unfolding causes and effects with meticulous care, as if he were excavating a great archaeological find. His superb handling of language and style, his paradoxes, aphoristic reflections and attitudes of aesthetic anarchism towards life and death all work together to produce a magnificent novel"

World Literature Today

"Helen Cavanagh's translation does full justice to the convoluted subtlety of this remarkable novel."

Peter Mackridge in the Times Literary Supplement

£6.99 ISBN 0 946626 74 X 128p B.Format